This Frozen World

This Frozen World

A Science Fiction Novel

BOB FREEMAN

Library of Congress Control Number: 2020910570

ISBN:	Hardcover	978-1-9845-8312-3
	Softcover	978-1-9845-8311-6
	eBook	978-1-9845-8310-9

Print information available on the last page.

Rev. date: 07/21/2020

To order additional copies of this book, contact:
Xlibris
1-888-795-4274
www.Xlibris.com
Orders@Xlibris.com
813999

FOREWORD

I have always believed that other planets circled our sun and that life on our earth came from one of those stars. This is a fictionalized story of how this all came about.

After reading, in my youth, "Buck Rodgers" and the origin of "Superman," I continued with that bit of day-dreaming.

This novel is the result of those dreams. It was prompted by the recent fear of global warming and its effect on the earth. Therefore, I took the liberty of changing the premise of a world destroyed by the alternate possibility. The results are this novel.

CHAPTER I

Dolf Frisca, President of Zavre United awoke to a dreary morning that prevented even the faintest sunlight to penetrate he and his wife, Angi's room. He immediately thought of the extra drinks he had at the previous night's dinner. It was a public relations task that he had to perform to attempt to pacify the governors of the various states who had cornered him requesting aid, financial assistance, and other items from the central government. Although his head was in turmoil, Dolf sensed an unusual darkening in his bedroom. At this time in the morning he would normally be greeted with sunshine coming through the curtains. All he experienced was a vague haze that had been occurring over the past months. *Was he imagining this?*

He immediately realized that this dullness in the sky, was getting more obvious during the last year. At this time, it was 7:00 AM. Normally the sky would be glowing and brilliant.

Drawing the curtains aside, Dolf could see the slight mist that had been evident for the last year. It seemed slightly deeper than before. The previous evening. he had been surrounded by the governors of various states requesting an opinion about his thoughts on climate change. *I have to get to the bottom of this,* he thought. And with this, Dolf Frisca threw on his robe and walked into his sitting room directly adjacent to the bedroom and there stood Zak Fellows his Chief of Staff with a tall glass of slightly warmed fruit juice. "How's our President this morning after an evening of drinking and carousing?"

"C'mon Zak, give me some room to breathe. I can stand the usual complaints about lack of services, foul- ups in projects and the typical political in-fighting, but they are getting to me with this mist thing. The pollution group are also getting a little more aggressive. They're now talking about temperature changes. I would have thought that this situation would have disappeared. but it hasn't. I can't avoid this anymore. I received an urgent call last night from Chad Asok, he said that the amount of energy some of his units are obtaining from the sun has been reduced and that he is considering closing down some power grids. This would greatly reduce our electrical availability. I need some answers as to what is causing this. Can you put together a short list of experts who can give me some answers within the next couple of weeks?"

"No problem, Mr. President, I'll get back to you by this afternoon with an appropriate list of candidates. It's probably nothing. Maybe a seasonal situation with dust blowing out of the North or temperature variations, but they'll get to the bottom of it. Now can we have breakfast? I have a half dozen requests that need your approval and signature."

#

Two days later, at ten o'clock in the morning, President Frisca sat at the head of his highly polished mahogany table, drumming his fingers, staring down at six of the most highly educated minds on the planet. Their backgrounds and experiences were as varied as were their ages and physical make-ups. They ranged from forty-five to eighty years of age with all holding doctorate and many other honored degrees from all the universities on the planet. Some were short, some tall, most over-weight from lack of exercise. The only thing they held in common was that they were all authorities in various fields of chemistry, physics, and other sophisticated earth sciences that he couldn't even comprehend no less pronounce.

Frisca, who felt slightly embarrassed with only his limited bachelor's degree, felt intimidated by this group. He took a deep breath and tapped with his pencil to secure order. It was recognized immediately.

"Gentlemen, I called you here this morning to present you with a problem that requires your immediate attention and your opinion. As you are aware, for the past months, we have been surrounded or perhaps more adequately put, enclosed in a slight haze.

"Although it probably is nothing of any consequence, its cause must be explained and resolved. At the monthly meeting of the state Governors held a couple of days ago, this situation was raised and I must get back to them with some answers. Before you bring up the subject, I am aware there is also talk about climate changes affecting temperature. Some towns in the North-west have been informed that their electrical supply from midnight to six AM could be reduced. They are obviously not happy with that news. Our wind turbines are doing fine but we are considering closing our least efficient solar farms." Frisca paused a few minutes to allow his guests to consider what he just said. He could tell by the expression on their faces they were not aware of the severity of this situation.

"I am asking you to investigate the cause of this phenomenon. You have unlimited funds and authority to secure this information. Dr. Chad Asok, who is sitting on my right, is my technical adviser on this project and will coordinate your findings. Use him to submit your results. Gentlemen, if there are no further questions, all I can say is: get me some answers."

#

It took six months, with various sub-committees begging extensions, their report came back. It was a massive document that Asok delivered to the President on a Friday morning with the comment, "Sorry, Mr. President, I've reviewed the complete report, it says nothing positive; nothing instructive. I'm afraid, Sir, we've wasted a couple of months without getting a definitive answer. I've taken the liberty of summarizing the report in a brief which is attached."

And so, finally, after months of fumbling about, with committees spending millions and not accomplishing anything, that afternoon, President Frisca called his Chief of Staff into his office, "Zak, call Dr. Andros at Jenwich and tell him I want to see him."

"Are you sure Boss this is the person you want?"

"Zak, give him a call first thing in the morning and get him over here. I've read some of his books and I think he may have the temperament and the brains to get to the bottom of this mess. I've spoken to a number of his associates and they say he is quite amazing." A phone call to Dr. Adam Andros was put through...a wiser choice could not have been found.

CHAPTER II

Adam Andros was the second born of a farm family living ten miles outside of the small town of Pensa. As all cities and towns on the planet it was a controlled town of 75,000, its population never allowed to vary by more than a few hundred. The Census Bureau maintained strong limits on the size and population of all cities and towns, and it was within those limits that Adam grew up.

At the age of three, his parents recognized his superior intellect. Not only could his parents sensed immediately that he was someone special---someone unusual. Adam identified the letters of the alphabet and could read newspapers that high school students would consider a challenge. He was reading when he was four and doing simple math problems when he was five. While his older brother, Crees, was interested in farm life, growing crops and water requirements, Adam was satisfied to sit on the porch reading about the moons circling the planet, thinking about what could be causing cloud formations and other scientific matters. Much to his parent's displeasure, he spent all of his free time in the library and spent all of his small allowance on science fiction magazines. Adam was admitted to the most prestigious school in Capitol City.

By his fifth birthday, the Education Department, realizing his unique talents with mathematics, enrolled him in a special school for those with his mind capability. By eight, when the department saw the results if Adam's exams, they were amazed. None had ever seen such results from one so young. His latent ability to solve complex math problems were far and away above all of those tested during the past twenty years. At fourteen he was recognized as a budding genius---a savant.

At sixteen, already completing his college requirements, Adam had already written two treaties on Zavre's possible formation Written by someone so young was also considered a remarkable accomplishment.

There his educational advisers soon discovered the extent of Adam's brilliant mind. He was head and shoulders above his fellow students in all matters scientific. His mind gobbled up and retained information that adults twice his age could not even comprehend. He developed the unique ability of being able to coordinate ideas and thoughts from one field of science to another. His mind saw areas of mutual compatibility and synergism that others failed to see.

On graduating at eighteen with his doctoral degree in astrophysics, Adam was offered a Adjunct Professorship at Jenwich University. Much to the horror of his advisor, he decided to specialize in astronomy and study the dead moons that were circling Zavre. When he completed his fourth treatise entitled, "Are We The Only Humans?" he was roundly laughed by his co-workers calling it "hog-wash", and rubbish. He became the laughing stock of the University but he could be happier. He published, at his own expense, a small monograph on scientific fiction, based on the general topics, "Can Life Exist On Another Planet." His writings were call, "science fiction at its worst." He accepted their ridicule with a shrug of the shoulders.

#

And then by happen chance his life changed six years later. He was twenty- six and resigned to his solitary life that he met Eve Matros. While he was having his usual synthetic meat dinner in the school diner and analyzing a complex mathematical equation that this attractive women, without any invitation, stood next to him. "Are you the infamous Adam Andros I've been reading about? I've been watching you for the past week, Dr. Adam, and I couldn't help but notice you eat the same food at every meal. Don't you ever consider changing your diet; even for one meal?"

Adam looked up to see who was giving him instructions on his strange eating habits. What struck him immediately were the brilliant blue eyes and fair skin of his adviser. "Well, dear lady," Adam responded, "I am perfectly satisfied with the same food every day and besides that I can't be bothered reading a menu. There are too many options. I get confused easily."

"Well, Sir, that's not what I hear," Eve answered, "if that is your only answer perhaps you will let me make your choice. I believe we have areas of mutual interest."

"Well let me decide that. What are you doing at the University?"

"I teach space exploration and astrology. Is that subject of interest to you?"

"It just so happens that it does. Sit down fair lady and we can share a drink and tomorrow you can pick my main course. Now tell me about any recent developments in your lab."

"Only if you tell me about the latest book you are writing."
"It's a short thesis about the possibility of a collision between two stars and the black hole. I'm sure you would be bored with it."

Eve smiled, as she answered, "you'd be surprised." She was in the process of writing a novel on that similar topic.

From that time, Eve choose Adam's menu as they discussed the latest in exotic scientific research over a wide variety of food preparations. Two months later, Eve, moved into his more exclusive apartment. They never considered a formal marriage arrangement would have any more binding affect than they were now experiencing in their mutual love of the sciences.

They had a synergistic affect on each others ideas, which aided in the discovery of two of the moons that circled their planet. Eve continued her deep space exploration while Adam took on the administrative problems. Eve's area of expertise was the ability to generate new concepts in examining inter-galactic origins. She had taken an advanced degree in astronomy and was considered an authority in planetary astronomy. Her background was in radio-wave research and prior to the misting situation she had spent most of her time searching for galactic noises that could possibly indicate other viable planets within their galaxy. Zavre had six small, uninhabitable moons in its galaxy, two of which they had been instrumental in discovering. The philosophical question had always been, "Are there any other livable planets?" Eve and Adam had spent many an evening discussing this possibility with no resolution. Adam had always felt there had to be something...someplace and if anyone knew where it was, Eve would know where to find them.

#

It was the following Saturday morning that Zak Fellows, following the President's requests, called Adam Andros.

After three rings a sleepy voice finally answered, "Yes, this is Dr. Andros's line. It's seven-thirty, you better have something important to say on our day off."

"I'm calling for the President. This is Zak Fellows his Chief of Staff. The President wants to see him this morning at nine. Tell him it is important."

"This is who?" Eve shook her head and sat up in bed. ""I may not have heard you right?"

"I'm calling for the President. I'm Zak Fellows. What is it that you don't understand? You know it's equally early for me. Tell Andros to be on time. He can have breakfast." No reason. No explanation. The phone went dead.

Lifting his head slightly off the pillow, Dr. Adam Andros muttered, "Who was that Eve? Do you know it's not even eight o'clock! We both had tough weeks; what was so important to talk to us now."

Eve, rolled over on her side, "I'm afraid you better get up. That was a call for you from the President's Chief of Staff, Zak Fellows. Have you been involved with him at all? Are you working on some strange project? They want you at the President's House at nine, so you better get moving. Take a shower and get moving. He said it was quite important. I'll talk to ya later."

"Did the caller say what this was all about?"

"I'm afraid not."

She turned over and closed her eyes planning to get another hour of dreams.

Adam walked to the shower, dropping his pajamas on the way. It was only under the beating hot water, that he finally realized what the telephone call could be all about— his only thoughts were, he hoped that it was not related to the haze problem. He had heard through the grapevine that there was no solution to that crises. All previous testing was not successful. He did not really want to work in a dead end battle. But, still why did it take them so long to contact him. His private research had done similar investigation and had come to a similar conclusion---it was the damn haze situation that was enveloping the planet. The President was finally going to inquire into its cause.

CHAPTER III

As the faint haze developed over the earth, with no logical explanation, most people considered it a minor hindrance, a temporary act of nature and nothing to worry about. Most of the scientists, when questioned, shrugged their shoulders and blamed the faint haze on the increased pollution on Zavre. During the year, Congress passed four bills attempting to reduce the amount of pollution that was allowed to be generated. The results were not successful. There were attacks on minority groups claiming they were the cause of the haze. Leading environmentalists joined in the fray pointing their fingers at everyone and everything. Industry was at fault, consumer spending, people's life styles and a dozen other causes offered no solution. In the halls of the Senate, debates were on-going about setting limits on pollution discharges. This caused an uproar as every Senator had a valid reason why the pollution laws should not be done in their state. Various sub-committees were formed but no uniform answer could be obtained. Each Senator had his or her own agenda and own interests to protect.

Years previously, the world of Zavre was all sun with a brilliant blue sky that hardly varied with the shift of the earth about its sun. Except for a two month period, in which the temperature was cool enough for the population to wear a light sweater in the evening, the temperature of the planet never varied more that fifteen degrees from season to season. Man had never given it much thought; for all recorded time, the sun had risen and set giving off its warmth and comfort. When it rained, and it only rained a couple of hours a month, it rained violently and with such force that all the cisterns and water reservoirs were filled for the year. Nothing varied. The planet's rotation about its sun was so perfect that only an hour was lost or gained in its 278-day trip,

Through this, the sun continued to shine, albeit with a slight mask; the minuscule decrease in temperature was barely noticed. The farmers were the first to notice the slight temperature decrease but their complaints and questions were ignored. The ice caps at the poles showed slight increases in size and depths as they expanded slightly. The Government spokespeople initially used legalese to explain the phenomenon, 'It is a temporary condition that would disappear.' Dissipate was a word they enjoyed using.

After all the talk about theoretical resolution of the fog, they were proven obviously wrong.

Adam thought a great deal about that day a year before. When he opened the drapes he noticed the faintest fog, or a veil of the most delicate lace that seemed to have descended over the sky. As he sipped his breakfast of enhanced vitamins and hormones in a warm juice base, he recalled his immediate thought was that it must have been caused by a dust storm in the desert some fifteen miles away. Perhaps, he thought, something was burning.

But when the news reports from his visual radio reported that the same weather condition was noted globally, he immediately, like the rest of the scientific community, thought that this was some type of pollution; but what pollution? There was no burning or use of biomass. Neither coal nor oil was used on the planet. Those types of energy sources had been depleted hundreds of generations before. Most energy was obtained from geothermal sources via long ceramic pipes set miles into the interior of the planet. These pipes, really huge conduits, had been set in place before anyone could remember. They extracted the unlimited heat from the interior of the planet, converting water into steam, which moved the turbines generating electricity. Additional sources of energy were thousands of gigantic wind-farms stationed on mountains that were so efficient that they supplied whole cities with electrical power. They were added by acres and acres of solar station situated at the right angles to obtain the maximum sun's rays.

The scientific world, at that time, could not conceive that it was not pollution caused by people or industrial pollutants.

In those early days, Adam and his co-workers underestimated the seriousness and the extent of the crisis. They believed it was a seasonal thing caused by pollution controllable by people and industrial plants.

CHAPTER IV

At five to nine, with the dampness of his shower still on his hair, Adam was met at the door of the Presidential house. Zak Fellows, a huge burley man, greeted him with a brief handshake, a sour face, and a few words, "I'm Fellows, I called you this morning. The President is waiting. You want juice or water?"

"Fruit drink would be fine for me. What is this all about, Mr. Fellows?"

"I'll let the President lay the problem on you himself." With that he opened the door to the President's small private dining room and departed, leaving Adam standing at the door entrance staring at the President. "C'mon in, Dr. Andros, I've been waiting for you. I hope Fellows didn't wake you, but we have to get to the bottom of this nonsense. Please sit. I guess Fellows went to get you some beverage. But let me start without him." As he was about to begin his words, Zak Fellows entered carrying a large pitcher of a fruit drink with a few glasses. He placed them on the table and sat down opposite Adam, hands folded nervously.

While Adam stared at the pictures of the last five presidents which adorned the oak paneled walls, the President swallowed the last of his sweet bun, finished his drink, wiped his mouth with a cloth napkin that was on his lap. "I hope you enjoy this fruit juice; it is my favorite. "Dr. Andros, let me skip the small talk and get right to the point as to why I asked you here. If you want anything else to drink please tell Zak, otherwise, I'll get to the heart of the matter." "That is quite alright,"Adam answered, "I am anxious to hear what you have in mind, although I can't imagine how I can be of service."

"Let me decide that, but I like your direct response, Dr. Andros; what's what I've been told about you…direct and to the point. But let me start my delima. Adam, I'm sure that you have noticed during the past year our planet's atmosphere seems to have been covered in a mist or fog. Our scientists thought this was a temporary thing that would disappear with a reduction of air-borne pollution or at least the rain or the wind. They thought as the planet went from one season to another, it was dissipate. As you know, that hasn't happened. Almost six months ago I authorized a select committee to study this problem. Over the past months the best scientists of the planet with the brightest minds have interviewed almost fifty people trying to understand what is causing this situation. They have conducted the most sophisticated tests and experiments and all I received was a document weighing five pounds telling me nothing."

He threw the huge manuscript in front of Adam. "Don't let this professional looking binder fool you; it gives no solution nor answers to our dilemma. All they have accomplished is to waste almost six months and fifty million quatros to discover nothing. Professor Asok, my techical advisor, reviewed their findings and his brief is attached. I believe I have correctly summarized all of their finding in two minutes."

Adam felt he had to interrupt, "Interesting, no one interviewed me for my thoughts."

The President laughed, "I can only assume that the chairman of the committee did not think that highly of you." "Thanks for that vote of confidence," Adam responded, with a forced smile.

The President smiled, ignoring the comment, and continued, "Our people are getting concerned about this misting situation. Part of the report states something about a decrease in the earth's temperature. Is that true? My question to you is what's goin' on? In a nutshell... get me the facts. When you read the small print of the submitted report you will see that the Industrial Council people are blaming the manufacturing plants. Waste disposal blame industry, and this repeats itself with everyone blaming another group. I need someone with no ax to grind, non- political, I have the confidence that you can accomplish this. I am appointing you to chair a committee to determine what is causing this. I do not expect you to turn me down!"

To ease his nervousness, Adam took a deep breath, reached for a juice goblet and poured himself a drink. He motioned to the two men if they wanted any, both nodded no. In his heart and soul, Adam knew that he was capable of heading this type of investigation, but, and this was a large but, was he able to control all the people whom he had to control? Many of them he would have to contact were egomaniacs and so self-centered that to control petty bickering he would need complete authority.

With those thoughts entering his mind, Adam charged forward, "Sir, I don't know if I should thank you for the responsibilities you have offered me but, I'm sure we'll find a workable solution to this unusual phenomenon. First, to be frank, I do not know why you chose me. I'm sure there are more qualified individuals in the world that could do this investigation. I could easily name four professors at Jenwich who could handle such a problem. Second, I am not sure that my findings and investigations will find anything different than your esteemed committee has found. Third, obviously I will require funding to conduct all the tests that may be required. Fourth, if I assume this responsibility, I must request that I have complete authority over the research and interpretation of our findings. Although I will set up various committees to advise me, I need final say. I need the final word. Working through committees may be fine, but very often they slow progress with the chairperson becoming too self-centered. I plan to keep you, or anyone you designate informed of our findings with the necessary reports, if you feel that is necessary, but I need the total backing and confidence of this office before I can proceed."

The President, after taking a brief sip from his drink, did not hesitate with his answer, "Adam. do not belittle yourself, we have chosen you after a great deal of thought and soul searching. I'd like to believe that what you will find is basically temporary and can be explained very simply, however I am preparing myself for the worst possible scenario. Although you have been delegated to a small lab at Jenwich University, your work on planetary exploration was well received in certain circles.. I was told that your monographs on possible life on other planets were ignored and much to your credit you had them self-printed. I read them with great interest. Although these short essays could be considered science fiction, the topics and the incidents that you describe may perfectly describe the conditions we may find ourselves down the road.

"I hope that your findings will not require such drastic action, but you never know what lies in front of you. The fact that your co-worker, Eve Masos, is a recognized authority on interplanetary travel and space exploration did not hurt your cause. I would expect that you would be using her on your team. Frankly, there are scientists with better backgrounds and experience from more prestigious sources than yours, but your ability to get to the bottom line and your administrative traits are what we were seeking. Why you were not chosen to be in the initial committee that met previously is beyond me, but that's history. Let's start with a fresh, new beginning. The information that I have previously received is informative and quite interesting, but it did not solve the problem on hand. In other words, I need someone who can give me an answer. I've convinced my advisors that you're the man to get to the bottom of this mess. I've already discussed this with Zak and you will have this office's full backing. Please send Chad Asok, your monthly or quarterly reports as you feel necessary. Chad is my technical adviser and should be able to interpret your results. He was a member of that select committee and should be able to assist you in any of the work that they had previously done. Adam, read the brief or the complete study and go to it— you have this offices complete authority."

Adam looked at the President with wide eyes, what could he say? "I gather I cannot refuse this job?"

The President, smiled, "I'm afraid it is written in stone, now get out of here and find out what the hell is goin' on."

Zak Fellows escorted Adam to the door as he whispered, "Get cracking on this, Doc, the population is getting restless."

#

On leaving the President's quarters, Adam knew immediately that he had to consult his best friends and authorities, in their own fields, about the project that he was assigned it. Eve, his girl friend and authority on astronomy would be needed for her expertise on space travel and Jonah Blanca, a school companion and friend for almost forty years was the most distinguished and honored scientist. A close personal friend of Adam and Eve, they knew each other since they were four. Although they had never worked together, they enjoyed each other's company and spent many an evening at dinners sharing common scientific problems. Only in his late 40's, twenty years previously Jonah had discovered a method to condense the size of batteries and make them more efficient. His miniaturized batteries were able to get many times the power of previous types. This technology was immediately put to use in the newer model cars and planes. As the daily papers simplified it, batteries that used to weigh one hundred pounds now weighed five pounds and their longevity was increased one hundred times; a most remarkable achievement.

It was a magnificent bit of research effort that was recognized throughout the planet and Dr. Blanca received every major scientific award. His picture appeared in every magazine and he was interviewed on every major TV program. Being single and unusually good looking did not hurt his image. Adam knew that the batteries currently used to propel the commercial airlines would have to be improved by one hundred or perhaps even one thousand times to even consider having the power to accomplish the purpose required. Adam also knew that if they were to attempt to escape from the planet's gravity, horse power would be a needed factor and no one on Zavre would know more about electrical generation than Blanca.

CHAPTER V

Adam and Chad Asok's first order of business was to review all the studies done by the previous committees. It took them almost a week to analyze their detailed results. Although they felt that their summary could not be rejected or ignored, Adam strongly felt that he and his newly organized commission should start from ground zero to obtain unbiased conclusions. He immediately saw that the President's summary was almost exact to the point. His comments were very disturbing. Chad backed away from the day-day activities as he was responsible to monitor the continuing reduction in the sun's rays.

Adam chose his committee carefully. Besides Jonah and Eve, he examined their obvious talents, education, and more importantly, their willingness to accept others opinions, however far-fetched they appeared. An open mind was by far the most necessary criteria. He did not want those individuals, however brilliant and usually too dogmatic and vocal, who would sit at his meetings, wring their hands with grief and moan, "For the good old days," or, "We should do things my way." The good old days had passed. "We must look to the future," was Adam's favorite comment. His next comment always was, "Think positively and look down the road."

Within a week, his first commission was delegated to analyze the causes of the misting. At their first meeting, Adam summarized the obvious: Would the ethereal mist that was covering the globe remain? What was causing it or of what was it composed? And of course, was the haze the determining factor causing the slight temperature decrease that the planet seems to have been experiencing? Adam had divided the research and investigation into two other groups; one, how could this mist be destroyed or controlled, two, how did it develop?

Within an additional two weeks, the research and discovery program went into effect. Experts in all areas relating to climate changes were contacted with the mandate to keep an open mind. Within their own fields of expertise they organized their own sub-committees to revise and summarize their knowledge of this strange problem.

Huge helium balloons were sent into the sky at various altitudes and then high flying planes were sent to obtain samples of this mist. At first it was like catching a cloud, a rainbow— but after many failures and modifications in technique, the ships came home with containers filled with something...at least something unique.

After additional weeks of intensive physical and chemical tests, they discovered that this mist was most unusual and unfortunately not able to be duplicated in any laboratory.

In layman's terms, the mist was a silica-organic complex whose structure was previously not even considered possible by the organic chemical experts. It consisted of an unknown molecule not described or envisioned in any chemical book in any library.

Basically, this report stated that the universe was enclosed in microscopic- sized particles of tri-valent silica molecules. These had been present since the planet was formed perhaps billions of years ago. What was now occurring was that pollutants, evolving from the world, were rising up like invisible fumes combining with the silica molecule and under the influence of the ultraviolet light from the sun, acting as a catalyst, producing this new reaction product that was shielding the rays of the sun from Zavre. It would seem to be unavoidable.

As described in the newspapers, this unique molecule was then shielding the sun's rays from the planet. The high polymer molecule was able to absorb and then retain the heat of the sun. It was, as one newspaper put it, "a growing monster with no body, no mind nor form." The government's Press Secretary was not happy with that comment and the reporter was seeking new employment shortly after his article appeared.

During the next six months, while the mist or haze continued its slow but seemingly inevitable growth, every major laboratory on the planet, with their research staff working twelve hour shifts, investigated this slowly growing problem. All their findings were filtered back to Dr. Andros and his now enlarged staff, who coordinated all the information.

Their reports were not encouraging; in fact they were frightening. The haze-mist could not be destroyed or reduced by ultra-violet or infra-red light.

Laser beams at all intensities did not seem to have any effect on its cross-linking ability. Radiation was considered, but discarded as being too dangerous to the population. Seeding of the atmosphere was considered but ruled inefficient. It would appear that this ever-growing menace was here for good. Another report on its sources was equally not appealing. Strong winds had little affect on the misting formation. They went through a rainy season with almost no change in the growth or reduction of the misting phenomenon. The third group's report was even more pessimistic; it was potentially fatal. The earlier reports and studies were confirmed: that the effects on the planets temperature were slow to develop but continued indicating some grave consequences. There was a very slight, but measurable decrease, in the average daily temperature. This committee was of the strong prediction that the decrease in temperature would increase exponentially over time.

Initially, a fraction of a degree per month did not seem overly catastrophic to the general population, but by using long-term models, the temperature loss caused by the inability of the sun to warm the planet would multiply geometrically and this would manifest itself by causing a decrease in the climate and growth conditions as well as increase in ice formations.

There were a few who disagreed with this prognosis and firmly believed that this temperature decrease was a natural event and that the planet had gone through these ice ages previously. When shown the studies of the intensity of the mist and its effect by the sun and corresponding earth's surface, and temperature of the ocean, they had to admit this was not a natural cycle of events. Using the most sophisticated mathematical models available, Adam's third group calculated that in twenty years the surface on the planet would be covered by one hundred feet of ice.

With the dismal and negative reports coming into the command central offices and laboratories of Dr. Andros, it was no wonder that he was reluctant to open the next fax or e-mail, or take the next phone call. His worst days began with a call from another university's research laboratories stating that current testing and examination of one aspect of the vapor problem had failed.... "What do you suggest— now?"

God, thought Adam, *what can I suggest? I am surrounded by hundreds of the greatest minds on the planet in all disciplines and we've run out of things to suggest.*

Some of their investigations were condensed in a four page single spaced report, others in a two hundred-twenty page thesis including pictures, graphs and charts. After taking a few days to digest all these studies, Adam called Chad Asok for a special meeting to discuss these findings. After reviewing all the reports, their opinion was unanimous, someone had to make a decision and inform the President.

CHAPTER VI

Every other Friday at nine-thirty, Adam would gather his team of experts in a small lecture room and review everything that had occurred in the previous week. This Friday, the meeting was different. Adam had asked all of his experts to bring in their immediate assistants and to be prepared to summarize their findings. Ocean temperature and weather changes, telescopic studies, chemical analysis, ocean depths, anything that could be related to the problem were reviewed for suggestions and possible exploration. The results were not encouraging. Average sea temperature was slowly dropping; the water levels were slowly receding from the landmasses, an indication of increasing ice growth, ice glaciers from the poles were measurably increasing, glaciers that were previously measured in inches were now feet and twice the depth. Plants were not germinating at their normal rates. The seasons which were normally stable were now undependable. Honey bees, usually a bell-weather for seasonal growth were late in their pollination habits. The requests for new thoughts, however bizarre, however wild, were not forthcoming. Adam glanced about the small room looking for someone to raise a hand for recognition with some new idea, new thought, but their faces showed nothing but a blank stare. The room became still… they had run out of ideas.

By eleven o'clock even the most optimistic Adam was depressed, "Gentlemen, ladies," he finally said after a long pause, "after the last report from Dr. Chenza's group on irradiation showing no progress and the slow but continuing decrease in the ocean's temperature over the past months plus those sections of our low lying cities experiencing water recession, we must consider the ultimate. We have run out of methods to control or slow this situation. The farm group's reports are equally discouraging. Agricultural production has decreased substantially over the past two years. Their report states that shortly we will have to grow all our food products under artificial means. Raising his voice to its highest volume, "Gentlemen, ladies, we must consider leaving the planet." Although the words caught in his throat, he had to repeat them, "We must consider leaving Zavre!"

The screams in the small auditorium became deafening. Half the audience was up on their feet screaming for recognition, while the other half was waving their arms, violently voicing strong objections and throwing questions into the air. "How are we going to do this? Do we have the capability?" and more distressing, "Do we have the time?" Adam allowed this utter bedlam to continue for a few minutes. Finally, he raised his hands and as the din subsided, continued, "I know this is not an easy or palatable decision to make, but someone must take the initiative. Your questions concerning our ability to take on such a task and those implications are well taken. We shall, during the next few months, investigate just those capabilities. Meanwhile, this is the decision I shall present to the President Monday at lunch. I intend to discuss our findings with the President and his staff and with Drs. Blanca and Masos. I suggest that the rest of you go to your offices and give me your opinions on this suggestion. A two-page summary, within your field of expertise, would be helpful and make my job much easier. Let me have this within the next few days. One thing, however, be positive and optimistic in your report. If we are going to be overcome by this natural calamity, let us use our ingenuity, let's go down fighting. Jonah and Eve, please come to my office."

An unusual silence filled the meeting room. Almost all of the scientists were afraid to admit that this, unfortunately, was the last resort, but privately most realized this could be the only solution, however dangerous and impossible it appeared. Most understood that with their current technology, they did not have the facilities for deep inter-space travel and if they did, where would they go? How they would accomplish this overwhelmed them.

#

Before Adam could corner his two associates, Dr. Samuels, past President of Zavre and in his early years a leading astrologist approached him, "Got three minutes, Adam?"

"For you, Dr. Samuels, all the time you need."

"I'm sure you noticed, Adam, that I sat in the back of the room not offering my opinion. There were times that I felt I could have offered some recommendations and comments but I allowed some of the young Turks to express their ignorance. I must admit, Adam, that your summary and answers to some of the questions were right on the money. I wish they were more positive or hopeful but you called them as you saw them. I pray that they could have been wrong."

"Dr. Samuels, I wish my summary would have been more hopeful, but the facts remain the facts...our planet remains doomed. Personally, I feel sorry for those few members of Zavre who will be chosen and expect to make the trip to another livable planet. They probably will be leaving their family, a planet with reasonably advanced technology and education for an unknown world. It is a frightening thought. I appreciate your calmness, under fire, I needed all the stable support I could get."

Samuels laughed and waved his walking stick at Adam. "I better leave you now before I ramble on as old men do."

Adam felt tears well in his eyes, Samuels was his first professor in college.

#

The lecture hall emptied much quicker than usual. They realized that time is a factor. Professors Blanca and Eve followed Adam to his office, their calculator brains working at maximum speed to prepare for all the possible questions they knew Adam was going to throw their way. At the meeting this morning they had already expressed their opinions and their thoughts on this matter; what more could Adam want?

CHAPTER VII

The three researchers quickly marched down the highly buffed wood floor to Adam's office. They stopped for a few minutes as Adam saw one of his junior associates and spoke to him about what was happening. With his arm about his shoulder, Adam exuded complete faith in his plan and Eve and Jonah could only envy Adam's confidence. Pictures on the walls of other scientists who graced these offices and laboratories and walked these halls seemed to grin and laugh at them as if their tasks were insurmountable. Adam tried to ignore their glances. Adams's secretary, Jebba, nodded at the two and handed Adam four faxes.

"I just received this information from Drs. Jesta and Okra. Their comments are not promising," she whispered.

Adam entered his inner office with faxes in hand. With Eve and Jonah watching, he opened the faxes, shrugged his shoulders and said, "Nothing we don't know already. The glaciers are continuing to build up on both poles. Within the last six months they have extended themselves an additional foot."

With those discouraging reports, both scientists entered Adam's office."What kind of office is this for a man with your responsibilities," said Jonah, as he made a face of what he saw. They had entered a small, one window cubicle containing three chairs, one behind a dark gray aluminum desk. The enlarged desk contained folders each marked with a different colored crayon to indicate its contents. The dull gray walls were lined with gun metal file cabinets some half open. Two pictures on the wall showed scenes of some distant mountains. The office was cold and unrewarding.

"Take a seat, Jonah," Adam responded, "this is a functional, working office not like your glamorous digs," they all laughed.

"Let's get back to the problem on hand. I wasn't expecting any block-busting news and these two faxs just conformed what I knew already, Jebba. I'll be having a brain washing session with Drs. Andros and Blanca. Stop all my calls. Bring in some drinks, we will need them. This meeting may last a while. I'll want you to join us to take notes. I may need those notes at further meetings with the President to defend my actions."

Before they even sat around Adam's extended desk, Jetta said," "The Chairman of the Astro-Physics Department from Simma wants to see you. He was at your meeting this morning and even before you got here he called to ask what your plans were for inter-space travels."

Adam laughed, "I only wish I had an answer to that one. I'll sic Dr. Eve on him. That should massage his ego and get him off my back."

The two guests sat in the uncomfortable chairs that faced the mammoth desk filled with reports, books and pictures. Adam sank into his seat behind the desk, cleaned an area immediately in front of him to get a better view of his visitors, and muttered, "Some day I gotta clean up this mess." Eve and Jonah smiled; their offices were in no better condition.

As they were waiting for Jebba to return with the drinks and her notebook, Eve asked, "When are you going to fax the rest of the investigators about your thoughts to get people off the planet? Shouldn't we alert them about your plans?"

"I don't think I should take that on myself. I'll speak with the President first; he's the one to make that decision, not me." They all nodded in agreement. "Secondly, I'd like to get your thoughts about feasibility. Which is why I have you here."

Fifteen seconds later Jebba entered the office carrying a tray containing a pitcher of water and four glasses. She placed it on a clean spot on the desk, invited the researchers to have a drink, but when they refused, sat in a rear chair, and opened a notebook, "I'm ready, Dr. Alexia, shoot."

Before Adam could open his mouth, Jonah started with a tone that showed a little annoyance. "Adam, we've been friends for years; we have told many a dirty story to each other, we have shared many a bottle of wine, but for the life of me I don't know why you have me here. We have just exited a meeting of the best brains on the planet who could not suggest a positive approach to our delimma and yet you have not invited those brainy people to join us. But no, you ask me and Eve, who by all votes, are not the smartest cookies. Are you playing games with us." He moved his chair as if to leave the room.

Adam's immediate raised hand response stopped him, "I chose you and Eve over the others because I have known you for years and I can depend on your imagination and imagination is something we may need a lot in this situation."

Jonah just shook his head in disagreement, "Adam, I appreciate your enthusiasm and I can see why the President has chosen you to lead this group. I still think you are taking the happy road to nowhere. You should know that your decision to leave the planet is at the best a wild one. We don't have the metal technology to build a adequate space ship. Special metals have to be employed. We don't have the capability via power source to completely escape the earth's gravity. Furthermore, to the best of my knowledge, I don't think we even have a destination. There are probably a dozen other reasons why we can't possibly make this journey and yet you suggest it. I think you're playing head games with the group." He paused for a second and then added before Adam could speak, "I think you are pulling their chains or worse, giving them false hope."

"C'mon, Jonah," answered Adam, "let's talk our way through this one. I didn't ask you to join us to wring hands. Let's see how this brain wash session goes. I need some ideas, I need some thoughts, I can only depend on you. Let me start with Eve and then I'll get you into the act, okay? Eve, have you found any response in the universe to your recent telescopic studies?"

Eve adjusted the neckline of her blouse, sipped some water, "Okay, guys, to appreciate what you are attempting let me give you a basic background of our solar system. Our sun is sounded by nine planets of which Zavre is a member. To put words to Adam's thoughts, his plan would be for us to to catch a favorable alignment with another planet and leave Zavre and start a new life on one of the other planet, hoping, no praying, that it's atmosphere matches ours. "I apologize Adam if I disclose your thoughts and ideas ."

"No, Eve, you have pretty well summarized my overall plan," answered Adam.

Jonah, who had been doodling in his notebook, "Eve, I must say your summary was perfect for a science fiction story, but how would we get to this other planet. By the way how far away is this closest planet?"

"Jonah, why do you give me the most difficult question, the closest is quite close but, unfortunately it is a dead planet. We could not survive there. The next closest one to us is one or two light years."

Jonah about leaped off his chair as he screamed, “We’ll be long gone by the time we get there.”

Eve raised he hands to stop Jonah’s further harangue, “Adam, I know I have told you this privately, I’m goin’ to repeat myself for Jonah’s benefit, but a couple of years ago, before this mist thing prevented my telescopic research, I was able to see pretty far in space and I have this feeling I saw something.

“Maybe I was lucky, but there could have been something in the quadrant I was scanning, I don’t know, I’ve been wrong before.”

“You haven’t been wrong too often in all the years I’ve known you.” Adam answered, “but what about your radio-laser wave studies— anything new?”

“Once again, and this is a wild guess, but I’d swear I got a bounce on my screen, a blip. I figure something in the South-South West about a couple of light years from us. Interesting, it came from the same direction as noted in previous reports from other laboratory electromagnetic spectra findings.” “So what you’re saying, Eve,” Adam broke in, “is that their may be something in our galaxy that we can travel to...another planet?”

“Holy smoke,” Blanca broke in, “even if we could travel at half the speed of light, which would be impossible, it’ll take us years. C’mon guys, a light year is six trillion miles. We could die in space if we had a way to get there.”

"Jonah, hold up your enthusiasm. Let's try to settle one crisis at a time. Eve, do you believe this is the closest thing to our earth, except, of course, our own sun or our dead moons?"

"Jonah at this stage, do we have a choice? In ten years, Zavre will be under ice." Adam took a deep breath, "Try to be optimistic, give me a guess."

Eve paused for a few seconds, while her two male companions squirmed in their seats. "Okay, if it's a guess you want, a guess you'll get. I think there is a planet or something out there maybe one or two light years away. Although I've been looking the whole 180-degree sky limit, when I return to the lab I'll concentrate on the area that showed the most promise. That will become my first and highest priority. As you are aware, I cannot do any further investigations with our telescopes; the misting has masked them. I'll have to rely on electromagnetic spectra techniques. I'll try to coordinate my findings with some other labs and see what they say. Perhaps, and only perhaps, by us working together maybe we can get more specific with our findings and location. I'm afraid this is the best I can do."

"Is it possible that the planets that you say you may have spotted shifted," asked Jonah?

Eve waved her finger at Jonah, "For a energy guy, you ask some astute questions, but you're right. Our galaxy is still expanding and in that expansion processes that planet may have moved a light year away from us.

Of course, trying to be positive, it could have moved closer. Let me throw something else into this mix. I've been doing some reading of old astronomy manuscripts and, believe it or not, in a hidden back room I discovered this report about the government, a hundred thousand years ago, sending a unmanned probe into space trying to discover some new planets. At that time they did not have the sophisticated techniques that we have now, but that flight was never heard of and they gathered that it blew up in re-entry. What they were able to decipher via their unsophisticated radio messages was quite interesting. However, that information was quickly forgotten. What did come back was that they discovered some life forms in an area of the sky we have never been able to rediscover. Their final report back to Zavre was that life could exist there, oxygen was the primary gas and the planet was covered with water, that's all we know. I guess the administration did not want to follow up on that report. Off the top of my head, I wonder if that space ship ever managed to find a habitable planet. I was impressed with this report and the mention of oxygen and water was quite impressive. An interesting thought, huh? Once again, it's a guess. Why they did not follow up on this exploration is strange, but something may have caused a stop to these explorations. Just don't use my name if you're going to publish this." Eve smiled.

"Don't worry guys, anything we discuss here will not be published or even discussed. Got that, Jebba?"

"Yes, Boss," was the immediate response.

Adam sat back in his chair and loosened his jacket. “Okay, however vague it may be, maybe we do have a destination. Now, let’s talk about power and energy to get us off this planet. How about it, Jonah, it’s your turn to expand our knowledge.”

“My God, I can’t believe what I’m hearing. Adam you must be off your mind,” Jonah immediately answered. “On some wild guess, you’re asking me to make some sort of statement on energy capabilities; no way, Adam. Sure my little batteries are efficient and small and they can supply short- term bursts of energy to run a car or a plane but the type of power that you’re requiring …never. Sure our planes can get to thirty thousand feet or so but within five thousand miles they have to land. It’s the same with our cars. Their batteries have to be re-charged every five thousand miles and they can only go eighty miles per hour. What you’re looking for, Adam, is in a different category. You cannot produce electrical power unless you have batteries the size of this room.” He sat back in his chair, exhausted. Jonah Blanca was not one to talk so much or so fast.

“And yet,” Adam interrupted before Jonah could add to his monologue, “your lithium-ion batteries reduced the battery size from a refrigerator to the size of your hand. Improve them another thousand percent and we are in business.”

“Sure...sure,” Jonah answered, “easy for you to say. It took us almost eight years of determined research to do that.”

Adam removed his jacket and placed it on the back of his chair. He filled one of the glasses with the drink Jebba had supplied. Those minutes gave him the opportunity to re-think his next approach. He knew before hand that this was the answer he expected from Blanca. But yet he knew, if he could present Blanca with a challenge he would not be the one to back away. He, of all people, would attack the problem with all his ideas and intelligence. Only then would a more favorable response be forthcoming.

"Jonah, that is just what I am expecting you to do. But let's get down to this case. How high can our planes fly right now?"

"They fly twenty to thirty thousand feet, but only for a couple of thousand miles before their batteries need to be regenerated. Every one of our airports currently has a regenerating station. There are no electrical outlets in space. Your needs are out of our league."

"Jonah, let me get back to Eve for a few minutes. Maybe then you can see an approach I've been thinking about. Eve, let me ask you another question.

"How high do we have to go to lose all gravity restrictions… to experience zero gravity? Is it fifty or one hundred miles?"

"I can't answer that question off-hand, Adam, but I'm sure it is less than that. Some of our space pundits would know that answer. I see where you are leading. If we can get a plane or some sort of a vehicle beyond the gravity of Zavre, at zero gravity, we wouldn't have a problem with speed. If we can get beyond gravitational forces we would be okay. The slightest push would throw us into outer space; an interesting concept."

"I hope so. Now back to you, Jonah. I hope you see where I'm coming from. Twenty years ago you miniaturized batteries, reduced their size, and gave them added power and longevity. Could you do that again? This time one hundred times? No, a thousand times. You would have unlimited funds and the best minds on the planet to work with. You need never complain about budget, equipment or manpower restrictions or about someone stealing your ideas."

Jonah rubbed his hand along his closely shaved face, and thought for a few seconds. He was never one to make rash or impetuous decisions. He pursed his lips and finally said, "Adam, as usual you're putting me on the spot. I doubt it, but it may be workable. We had been using a nickel-hydride combination which gives us the energy that we need. Before this misting mess took up all of our time, we were experimenting with some new lithium cobalt metal complexes coated with new synthetic plastics. The combination seems to have electrical staying power and they could be miniaturized. But with it all, this still would not give you all the energy to escape Zavre gravity. For short spurts we may generate enough power, perhaps five hundred horse power, but that's all. A space ship that you are considering may weigh hundreds of thousands of tons. To have the power to move such a vehicle will require awesome power, perhaps ten thousand horse power"

"Jonah, let's not disregard short spurts of energy. This is what we may require"

"I understand where you are coming from Adam, but at this time all we have been able to achieve is a short burst of energy. Long term energy shocks are out of the question. See my dilemma?"

"Jonah, but that's the rub," Adam immediately responded, "all I would need is a short energy boost." He rubbed his big hands through his hair, my thoughts are," Adam continued, "if we can get to maximum altitude with some type of space ship, say sixty to seventy miles and then, with an extra burst of energy from your new batteries, it would throw the ship out of the gravity limits of the planet and then into deep space. Once we eliminate the gravity constraints of the sun, the slightest push should move us in the direction and speed we need. What I am considering is that we go out into space as far as possible, travel around our sun, trying not to get pulled into their gravity forces and then, as we spin around, we give one final blast with our new found energy boosters to get into outer space. The sun would give us enough momentum to push us on our way. As I see it, we use the sun to give us that extra push to free us. Do you think that could be a workable concept?"

"You do realize, Adam, that the sun would also want to pull you into its gravity field— into its orbit," Eve interrupted. "We could be burned up just as easily."

"I know that," said Adam, "we'd have to be on the very edge of the sun's attracting range. It wouldn't be easy, but our pilot would have to be aware of that. We'd have to get the best pilots on the planet to pull off such a maneuver, but we can pick and choose the best. I'm sure we'll have that authority." Both Jonah and Eve looked at each other incredulously.

"My God, Adam, as crazy as it sounds, it might work at that," Jonah finally said with a grin. "You do realize that this ship of our will have to have special heat shields. If we get too close to the sun we could be burned alive. We also would need cooling devices for re-entry, if we ever get that far."

Adam tented his fingers, "No one said this will be an easy engineering job, Jonah. We'll need the very best airplane manufacturers on the planet. I am aware that this ship will require special equipment and structure that will be new to us. But that is why you are here. What do you think, Eve?"

"It's an interesting idea. But to be frank Adam, we don't have too many options. There'll be a lot of work to do, but I'll be here to tell you in what direction to go. At least I'll have a job for the next couple of years. It's better than sitting around and waiting to freeze to death. You guys realize there is going to be a clothing shortage in a couple of years. We're going to make a lot of engineers unhappy leaving their current job and joining us."

With the comment, Jonah started to laugh. "What's so funny," asked Eve.

"I was just thinking, if we leave the ship wearing face masks and our normal wear and there are any people on this plant, they will believe they are being invaded by aliens."

They all laughed weakly. Finally Jebba said, "Its twelve-fifteen, your guests will be here shortly."

"Before we break up this party," Adam continued, "Jonah, besides your normal duties of overseeing the battery research and progress, I'd appreciate if you would coordinate the engineering work that will be done to build some sort of a space ship that will meet all our requirements. Number two, I will not have the time to keep reins on the ship building people as I have to take care of the food requirements and the administration part of this program. And three, I am not familiar with the coordination of energy and the size of the ship and its requirements. After I see the President and if I get the go-ahead, let's get together and discuss this situation."

Adam rose slowly from his chair. "I better be able to sell this idea to the President, although I don't see where he has a viable choice. I hope you guys will excuse me, I have some people to contact."

"What is your first order of business, Adam?"

"First to see the President and get his approval to continue on this project and second, to look for someone who can supply us with a food source to last maybe ten years. Third, an engineering company who can build us a plane that can tolerate space travel. Now that's an interesting problem."

"Good luck, then Adam," answered Jonah, as he walked out the door with Eve.

CHAPTER VIII

For the next two days, all Adam received from his subcommittees were negative responses saying his thoughts and plans on inter-space travel were not feasible. Their next comment was, "Good luck." Time had gone so quickly that he had not the time to get clearance from the President. Adam finally called the President's house and Zak Fellows picked up the phone.

"Mr. Fellows, this is Adam Andros, I would like to speak to the President about the project he gave me. I think it's time for my associates and I to have a one- on- one discussion about our discoveries and thoughts on this misting question. I also would like his suggestions and go-ahead on what we propose."

The response was immediate, "Thanks for the call, Adam; the President would like to see and talk to your people. He's been waiting for a report. We'll be having lunch in ten minutes, can you join us?"

"We'll be there in fifteen minutes," Adam answered.

On the run, the three scientists were out of the research building and on the electric bus that traveled its route around the Capitol. Within fifteen minutes they were at the President's house and were immediately ushered through the various waiting rooms into a small private dining room in which the President held his intimate get-together. The President, Chad Asok and his Secretary of State, Zak Fellows, were already standing in a corner sipping red wine and nibbling on some delicious looking canapés. The Secretary looked at his watch as the three entered the room; they were a little late.

Adam, Eve and Jonah approached the small, elegantly appointed table. "Sorry, Mr. President," said Adam, "We were delayed by traffic. These are my two closest researchers, Professors Eve and Blanca, who will be coordinating various aspects of this project. I have brought with me copies of the summary of my committees comments of the problem we face. I'm sure all of your questions will be answered in this report but do not feel that your additional questions will not be appreciated."

The President nodded his feline head briefly at Eve and Jonah in greetings and continued, "Adam, time is gold for me, be prompt the next time." He was obviously annoyed. "This is my scientific advisor, Chad Asok and Zak Fellows, my Secretary of State. You have already met them. Sit down, people. I've ordered a glass of red wine, my favorite; I hope you'll enjoy it." Like all professional politicians, President Frisca's frown had changed to a broad and sincere smile. He had made his point, and now that he was back in control, he could be the ever-pleasant host.

After the wine was served and lunch was ordered, the six shared small talk about local gossip and current political manipulations. Adam sat back in amazement that with the critical nature of this meeting, lunch was progressing as if the world were going along as usual. He could not believe that with the life of the planet at stake, these three could be so nonchalant. He only assumed that Frisca and his associates did not realize the magnitude of the catastrophe that lay ahead.

After lunch and the drinks were served, the President loosened his tie, removed his jacket, which he hung behind his chair, signaled to the waiters to leave the room and in his deep melodious voice started, "Adam, Dr. Eve and Dr. Jonah, let's get down to cases. If I recall, it was almost a year ago that I asked Adam to find out what was causing this misting-fog that is affecting our planet. Much to Adam's credit, he has been sending me timely summaries concerning his group's studies. Dr. Asok, here, has been deciphering those reports and we both agree the results are very disturbing. That is the first issue. The second issue, and the most important one, is that the country is getting paranoid. They are getting worried and I can understand it is my responsibility to tell them what's goin' on. There has been unrest in some of the smaller cities in the Northwest. The people in the farmlands have been especially vocal. We've tried to keep our information under wraps by down-grading the causes but I'm sure it will continue and get worse. I know that you fellows have done a lot of homework on this problem but other advisers have been giving me some conflicting summaries. Adam, I'm glad you called for this head-to-head so we can get to the bottom of this and explain the situation in language we can understand. So, Dr. Andros, be brief, be exact with your words and as harsh and truthful as you need to be." Frisca looked at Adam, Jonah and Eve with a look of exasperation.

Adam could see immediately why Dolf Frisca could be the President. In perhaps seventy-five words, he had summarized what he wanted to know. Adam hoped that he could respond in kind.

Adam took a deep breath and began, "Mr. President and gentlemen, I asked for this meeting as our research committees have completed their study of the cause of the misting problems that has covered our earth for the past year or two. To put it in a few words, the world is in a catastrophic crisis. Because of the haze that we've been experiencing, the sun's heat has not been able to reach us, causing global cooling. As I have said in my reports, we have explored all normal, and some abnormal means, to eliminate or even reduce the hazing problem with no success. Our planet continues to get cooler, albeit slowly. This cooling is slow but inevitably will cause ice to cover the globe. The whole planet will be under glaciers within ten or twenty years. There seems to be no way of turning this off. Life on this planet, unless you are a polar bear, cannot survive." There was a slight smile from the six of them. "This will be an ice age to beat all ice ages. If that's an exaggeration, it's just a small one. I say all these negative words with due diligence. This is the summary of all of our top scientists.

The six around the table sat in deathly silence for a full thirty seconds, thinking their own personal thoughts. The only sound heard in the room was the clicking of the secretaries heels walking in the halls outside the office. Adam realized that it was utterly impossible for them to grasp completely the words that he had just said.

"With all that bad news, let me tell you that a number of our scientists are considering the only alternative, and that is some of us leaving Zavre. At this point in time, it may be beyond our current capability, but it is a slight possibility. If nothing else, it gives us a ray of hope beyond this darkness. Mr. President, we require your approval so that we may go ahead with our plans as rapidly as possible." He took a deep breath; he said what he had to say.

After a few throat clearings, Chad Asok entered the conversation. "Adam, I have re-read the summary of the reports from your various committees. As part of one of the sub-committees, I disagreed with some of their thoughts. I must commend you however on their thoroughness, but I still feel there are a few questions that should be clarified. I may be out of turn and the answer may be in your report, but I've been in touch with some of our leading astro-geologists. They claim, and I am aware that you may have already considered their opinion, that this cooling episode is not caused by the misting but by a slight shift in the axis of our planet. Our planet seems to have a slight wobble every two to three-hundred thousand years or so which causes a cooling of the planet. This causes a temporary ice age, which is something that has occurred previously. Adam, can you comment on this statement?"

"You raise an excellent point Chad and we have closely examined and reported on that possibility. There is a shift of this planet every thousand years, but the cooling dilemma that we are now facing is not caused by that, it is caused by a chemical reaction taking place in our upper atmosphere. This chemical reaction is not reversible and is preventing our sun from warming our planet causing the misting that we are experiencing. I wish it were otherwise. The bottom line being, as Dr. Blanca may add, life on Zavre is limited to ten or perhaps twenty years."

"Is that the time limits you foresee?" Chad Asok asked, quizzically.

Jonah answered, "Allow me to answer for Dr. Andros. This is the maximum time we see in our calculations, although we are guessing in the spirit of caution. Furthermore, when the ice formation reaches our underground heat sources there can be a massive eruption that could blow the planet apart prior to its being completely frozen. This is a scenario which some of our people feel is a good possibility." Adam and Eve glanced at each other. This was something they hadn't even planned to bring to the table.

With an attitude showing his disbelief, Chad Asok had to show his negativity to the whole concept, "If we further tighten up our pollution laws perhaps we can delay this catastrophe from occurring during our life time. In one hundred years our scientists could resolve this situation. Could we use the heat from our heat conversion plants to hold off this temperature drop? Maybe we can slow our time of ruin?"

"A very good thought," interrupted Jonah, "we have considered that possibility among a hundred others but that would only be temporary with the ice rising a hundred feet above the surface of the planet. We may be able to delay but we can not stop the inevitable. Zavre will be a dead planet like other moons within twenty years, if it doesn't first explode.

"Remember, five hundred years ago we were not generating the quantity and density of pollution that we are producing these days. Our report gives, in detail, the tons and tons of pollution we are generating, but consider that as we burn this trash it escapes into the atmosphere. The discovered molecule that is formed is causing the misting to retard the sun's rays from reaching us. Our planet, very shortly, will be enclosed in an increasing envelope of mist. This situation is not a cyclical event."

Asok went on with his questioning, "We just went through our rainy season. How did the rainstorms affect the misting and fog? Did the rain disperse this cloud cover? Did your people see any changes in the intensity of the mist after the rain?"

Blanca raised his hand to prevent Eve and Adam from responding, "Dr. Asok, that is a great question and we were hoping that the rains would help our situation as it had in past history. In fact, it did, but a minimal amount. Our labs around the world, measuring the intensity of the mist after the rainy season, all agreed it was reduced by no more than two to five percent, not enough to solve the greater problem. The temperature continued to decrease as the weather cleared."

Once again, Asok had to ask, "How slowly is the temperature decreasing. Is it noticeable?"

Waving off Eve, "Let me handle this one," said Jonah. "Basically, at this time, the decrease in temperature can only be measured in half a degree. But down the road the temperature will slowly decrease a full degree. Not significant to you but vital to the farmers and their growing season. Our growing season for food will slowly change. It will also cause greater formation of ice at the northern and southern poles. The level of the ocean will drop as the ice increases. Secondly, our population, within a short time period, will realize, if they haven't already, how cool and then how cold it's becoming."

President Frisca took a deep breath, and answered, "This all doesn't sound good. Where do we go from here? Do you guys have any optimistic ideas that I can pass on to the people? You may not be aware that the suicide rate is up, and crime has increased. As I have previously said, there are increased reports of rioting in some of the small towns. I'm considering declaring martial law. I have to tell the people something.

"Adam, you haven't said a word," after a pause for a final sip of his drink. "What is your opinion, what are our options, your thoughts?"

"I'm afraid my thoughts are more devastating than my associates. I have reviewed all the summaries from the best brains in the universe and their comments are consistent; this planet is doomed. Except for a small number of non-believers who will reject anything scientific, the consensus was our opinion was correct. I realize that it's a horrible word to use, but it summarizes our conclusions. Our only hope is for some of us to try to leave the planet while we still have the opportunity and while we were still able to explore the atmosphere with our electro-magnetic radio waves. It appeared that there might be another planet within our galaxy that has our sun with the needed atmosphere to survive. If you require, Eve can fill you in on the specifics of that research. At this point in time, she is trying to pin down that blip on her screen that gives us some hope. Second, Dr. Blanca will be working on an energy source that will get us out of the gravity constraints of this planet. If that research is successful we may have the ability to leave the planet. The bottom line Mr. President, is I need your approval to go ahead with this project. I must have full authority to obtain the necessary funds, hardware and people to go ahead with such a plan. We realize that it is a long shot, and it is a faint possibility. To summarize all of our talks is that we don't have any alternatives."

For an awkward few minutes the table was quiet as the President got off his chair and walked to his window and stared out. The grass on the wide lawn was a deep shade of green. His mind thought, *how long will that last.* "Tell me. Dr. Andros. How many people do you believe you can remove from the planet. We must try to remove a considerable amount otherwise we would have not accomplished anything."

Adam's answer came quickly, perhaps too quickly, "To tell the truth Mr. President, at this time we have no idea on how many citizens we can save. It would depend on a dozen factors of which we have not considered. All I can say is that we shall aim to remove as many as possible, but please consider one hundred to five hundred and I am only guessing. That number will be strictly dependent o the batteries that Jonah's people can devise and the size of the ship our engineering people can design. " He looked quickly at Jonah.

"Mr. President, Jonah immediately interrupted, "I think Adam is a little premature with his numbers. We will not have any ideas of the figures for awhile. As a good administrator he is awfully optimistic. I will keep Dr. Asok informed as to how that progress is going."

Returning to his seat at the table and his visitors, he stared at his hands and finally, in a voice so low that they had to lean forward to hear, "I don't know if I can give you carte blanche without further discussion with Congress, but within my limits you have it. That's it? I do not think I need a review by Dr. Eve. You pretty well answered all the questions I would have asked."

Frisca rose from his chair, put on his jacket and with sadness in his voice said, "Do we have a choice? I'm sure there are dozens of issues that we will discuss down the road, but we can get to them later. Right now, Adam, you have authority to continue your research and your exploring. Do not limit yourself to funds and manpower; contact your people. Keep me or Dr. Asok informed as to your progress. I know we'll talk again and soon." He reached across the table and shook hands with Eve, Jonah and Adam as he and his associates left the room. Adam was to say, much later, that he saw a mist in the President's eyes.

On the way back to their apartments, Adam turned to his friends, "I guess, guys, it's time to stop the talk and get to work. Tomorrow morning get on the phone and start the program rolling. I'm sure time will be a factor down the road, so let's start moving. Jonah have breakfast with me tomorrow morning, I have the feeling that finding a company to build a ship to meet our needs will not be easy."

#

That night, and the proceeding days and nights following, Frisca spent his available time with his advisors and his cabinet discussing how he should present the drastic news to the population. Should he come on strong indicating no hope is to be expected. Announce that a space ship is currently being considered or the worst scenario tell the citizens to contact their drug suppliers and request mild poisons. Frisca tried to take the advice of his advisors but knew he was the only one to make such decisions.

#

A month later, President Frisca made a speech heard by 85% of the population. Choosing his words very carefully he stated that there was a problem with the cloud cover that was affecting the earth's temperature. All avenues of research were being explored to solve the situation. The best minds were working on all areas that showed some progress. He briefly mentioned that thoughts of building a space ship was under consideration. He closed his up-beat speech that he was sure that the catastrophic events would be resolved by the fertile imaginative minds of man.

Adam looked at Eve who whispered, "I guess he's speaking about us. I wouldn't want to be in his shoes."

Adam answered, shaking his head, "I wouldn't want to be in mine."

#

The following weeks, Adam's phone, fax and E-mails were swamped with messages from everyone on the planet. Between trying to line up contractors to solve potential problems and contacting known authorities in the field of manufacturing requesting recommendations he was obligated to answer some of the questions they asked. Although many were pertinent and to the point others were insulting, blaming him and his "egg heads" for causing all this "mischief." They could not believe the situation as presented by the President could be true. Why were they not consulted for their views on this situation? It was difficult for Adam to maintain his dignity in responding to some of these questions.

His responses after a long day on the phone were usually,'contact your representative or we are still working on various solutions or, the worst, have faith.' Adam knew that these responses were a cop-out, but he hadn't had anything else to say.

#

It was a week later with the temperature a shade cooler than to be expected at that time of the year, Adam was just about to put on his warmer jacket and leave his office for a meeting with one of his sub-contractors when Jetta knocked on his door, opened it slightly, placed her head inside and in a barely heard voice whispered, "President Robinson is in the waiting room and would like to have ten minutes of your time."

Adam sat back on his chair in amazement, Robinson was at his last meeting and is aware of what is going on. *The President of Jenwich requesting time from me? How could I refuse."* Please send him in, Jetta."

Within five minutes, Robinson hobbled into Adam's office on his decorated cane and without a word of greeting sat down on one of the chairs facing Adam. Placing his cane between his knees, he waved off Jetta's offer for a drink and began.

"Dr. Andros, I cannot imagine the problems that faces you, but that being said, please give me a few minutes to express my thoughts. I have taken the time to completely read and evaluate the future of our planet. For the last couple of months, I've been trying to obtain more information as to how many passengers this proposed space ship may carry and secondly who will choose those passengers. Surprisingly no one in the administration wants to answer those questions. I listened very carefully to Frisca's speech the other month and although it was a masterpiece of semantics, I do not feel comfortable with all of his answers. Now, I must admit I am an out of date scientist, in fact I could barely understand some of the points made in the study, but I still have faith in our people. But let me be more specific, I cannot believe that in the technological world like Zavre we could not beat and solve this cooling situation. Did we not eliminate 90% of the common diseases? Didn't one of your researcher friends invent new energy techniques? Did we not put together our remarkably efficient wind farms and control our tidal waters with our creative engineering and generate tremendous amounts of power through those sources. Have you explored the possibility of reducing the continual build up of the mist by controlling industrial and human pollution? Over the past one hundred years the longevity of our population has increased by almost ten-fifteen percent. My bottom line being our people have solved the unsolvable problems that had haunted our ancestors for hundreds of years. We have faced these challenges before and succeeded.."

Adam smiled at President Robinson's naivety. He did not believe it was necessary to repeat the summary of the report outlining the cause and the result of the global cooling. All of Robinson's comments were correct and had been considered and discussed.

It was quiet in the room, as Robinson wiped his forehead with his handkerchief. He hadn't spoken so forcibly in years. Adam had really nothing to say or add, finally some nondescript words emerged, "President Robinson, I cannot disagree with your comments but the facts are there ...it is obvious that a calamity will occur to our planet within our lifetime. As you heard at our last meeting all of our most concerned scientists and engineers have concluded that this is not science fiction. You and all of our participants at our meeting received a summary of their opinions. We have considered all of your points and although we agree with them we cannot avoid reality. The bottom line is harsh but it is truthful. President Robinson, I apologize, but it is the only answer I can give you. To be repetitious, within fifty years there will not be a living person on Zavre."

Robinson nodded his head, took hold of his cane and without another word left his office. Adam put is head in his hands and whispered, "*Oh my God.*"

CHAPTER IX

Seven weeks later, Jonah and Adam were ushered into the exclusive office of Davis Engineering. Both President and Vice President, Ezra Davis and Ruben James, jumped to their feet and with some slight insincerity in the voices, stuck out their hands, "Welcome, Gentlemen, we are glad to see you at this time. This is a a busy time of the year for Davis. Please be seated, may I offer you a drink? What can we do for you?"

Jonah and Adam looked at each other in amazement, they would have thought that Davis and James would be aware of the reason for this visit. They both turned down their offer of a beverage. This was to be a business meeting and could prove to be very sensitive.

Davis and James's joint office was a perfect example of the result of two outstanding students who had inherited their parents lucrative and well managed business. The twenty by sixty foot office, paneled in a rich, dark mahogany was interspersed with book shelves filled with original signed novels and plaques and statues indicating the company's donations and good deeds to various organizations. It was an outstanding office and Adam was duly impressed.

Ezra started the conversation with some hurried words, "Dr. Andros, as Ruben has said, 'we are extremely busy.' Davis is currently involved in the completion of two ships. One is 90% completed and the other has just been wired and on our production line. I hope your visit here don't refer to our work force or future production plans. We have already invested almost five million quatros on these projects. We are currently working on two other contracts."

Jonah looked at Adam with some reluctance, he was not the one to get involved in a word argument. Fortunately, Adam picked up the gauntlet. "Mr Davis, Mr. James I am here at the direction of the President and with his complete authority." He removed from his inner pocket an official letter signed by Frisca and countersigned by Fellows giving Adam and his associates complete authority over all building and plane construction at Davis Engineering. "Gentlemen, as of this moment all commercial production and research will be directed to build a space craft to move citizens of Zavre off this planet. Jonah will be my coordinator at Davis and keep me abreast on all of your activities and progress. I am really sorry, but if you would have heard the President's speech the other week, you would be aware of the desperate situation we face and the need to take this extreme measure. In short, all your production and research shall now be directed to the manufacture of a space ship that will meet all of the requirements of inter-space travel. We are terribly sorry if we come on to you so strongly, but the situation that is affecting the planet can't be handled more delicately. This project must have first priority."

Ezra Davis sat back in his chair as if shot with a bullet. "I heard Frisca's speech and really thought this was a PR gambit getting Frisca some additional votes for his election next year. I could not believe what he said was the truth. We really thought he was exaggerating this fog situation. Where have you guys been for the six months."

Jonah interrupted Ruben on coming questions, "Gentlemen, for the last months we have been interviewing every major ship and plane manufacturer. We have visited all the railroad car manufacturers, every builder of heavy steel and metal products on Zavre. Amazingly enough, Davis Engineering's name led all the rest. It appears that Davis has the best reputation and ability on Zavre to manufacture what we need and what we require. We need your company's talents. You've been elected. I have to say that all the planes you currently have on the delivery line have to be converted to meet inter-space travel."

Ezra Davis and Ruben James stared at each other in amazement. Their tongues stuck in their mouths. How could they answer this challenge."Let me jump in here," Adam butted in, "We realize that the task laid before you is unimaginable but you will have complete authority to pirate any aero-engineer, metallurgist or authority in this field you want. Any piece of equipment that you feel will assist you in this program is yours! Costs should not enter into your research or building. Gentlemen, we expect your 100 % cooperation. You already have the governments."

After a few minutes of embarrassing silence, Ezra asked, "I guess we have to remove two semi-complete ships off our production range?"

"Only if their basic structure cannot be used in inter space travel," answered Jonah.

"We will have to re-write our blueprints to consider aerodynamic requirements," Ruben James immediately answered out loud. "As responsible for all production at Davis, I will have to have my engineers redesign a ship to meet the requirements of space travel something they have never done. Do you have any idea how large these planes should be. How many passengers do you expect to carry on these ships. That information will be vital if we are to meet specifications and a delivery date."

Both Adam and Jonah shook their heads in agreement.

"My friends, you'll have to do what you have to do." The answer to this question was obvious. We will get back to you as soon as possible."

"How soon will we start to feel the affect of the climate change," asked Ruben.

Adam was ashamed to answer, "According to our experts, it is currently happening, but in slow motion. Our meteorologists tell us the results will be obvious in one to two years."

Ezra responded, "I guess it could take almost that long to put together a vessel to withstand all the problems of outer space. Will Jonah be working on power sources? We will need much more than we currently have."

Jonah's response was to be expected, "You and your engineers will be seeing me almost every day to coordinate our results."

And with those words Jonah and Adam left the office of Davis Engineering.

CHAPTER X

A week later, Jebba contacted Adam on the intercom, "Drs. Loren and Able are here. They indicated that you called their office for them to see you. I don't have them down in your appointment book."

"Sorry, Jebba, I must have called them directly and never told you. Tell them to come right in."

Within seconds, Loren and Able entered Adam's office and were ushered to seats facing his desk filled with files of information on current progress from his various groups. None were overly optimistic. Loren and Able were the epitome of what successful chief executive officers should look like. Impeccably dressed in tailor made suits that reeked of money, which could have paid for a year of Adam's tuition in graduate school, they were tanned and fit, showing many an hour spent in the spas and massage parlors. Perfectly coiffed hairstyles fit their square-chinned faces. Adam envied their savoir-faire and grace.

"Gentlemen," Adam started, "thank you for responding to my urgent call so rapidly. I realize how busy you fellows are and I appreciate your time, but almost two months have passed since the President's speech and we have to move along with this project. Not to mince words, I need your help on a major product that I believe only your company can make."

Jackson Loren, the senior of the two, raising his hand to stop of Adam's conversation, responded immediately. "Dr. Andros, we are aware of the climate changes that are occurring on the planet and our investigators have told us that you have top priority from the government to secure anything you require. Money is not to be an issue. Bottom line: what can we do for you? But to be frank, I'm surprised that you did not contact us before."

"Dr. Loren, thanks for your frankness, but prior to contacting you, we had to evaluate and consider all the companies on the planet to accomplish what we require. First and foremost, we had to determine if their was a manufacturing company that could build a space ship to meet the needs of outer space requirements. Without which this whole project would not exist. We hope we have accomplished this. and we are now on the next order of priorities. It seems that what we require can only be produced by your organization. My staff has done some investigations and the consensus is that your company, Corporation Drugs, is the leading manufacturer of pills, tablets and supplements. Your organization also has the most advanced laboratory to develop new products. It is in that area that I require your help."

Dr. Abba Able smiled at those words, "I wish you wouldn't tell our competitors that, but you are right. We are very proud of our reputation. What type of pills or supplements are you seeking?"

"Excuse my naivete and my ignorance, but we will require a food supplement that would give a human enough energy to last a couple of days.

It would have to be incorporated into a pill or a tablet. If it could be incorporated into a liquid form that too would be acceptable. Is that possible?"

Being polite, both Doctors hid their smiles as well as they could. After a brief second of looking at each other, Dr. Able answered, "One tablet to give all the energy and nourishment for a human for a day would have to be the size of a baseball; how about two tablets a day?"

Adam rubbed his hands together, "We could consider that." He tented his fingers for a second and then continued, "What I envisioned, or hoped for, is a food supplement that is readily digestible and that would not cause any gastric problems. Hypothetically, suppose we would require, lets say, a million pills that would meet those requirements. How much would they weigh? How long would it take to make that quantity?"

"Dr. Andros, let's put things in the proper sequence," Dr. Loren responded, "First, we'd have to find if we could formulate such a tablet. Second, we have no idea, at this point in time, of its possible size and third, its weight could only be determined by its efficacy. Fourth, we would have to re-design our machine molds to produce such a tablet. How long would it take to make? Let's do first things first. Let's see what our research people can come up with. We have some clever people who may be able to give you what you want. Sound like a plan?"

"A great plan if it works; can I have updates on your progress every couple of weeks and a resolution in a couple of months?"

"Dr. Andros, you are putting us on a time table that we may not be able to meet. Zak Fellows, the President's Chief of Staff told us that you are a result-orientated guy. We just didn't believe that you're that go-go. This project that you put us on could take a couple of years. Under normal circumstances it would have taken five years."

Adam took a deep breath and exhaled deeply, "Gentlemen, I wish I were able to give you that time to solve this problem at your normal pace. I don't have that prerogative. Speed is essential. If you spoke to Fellows you are aware of the time restraints under which I am working. I'd like to have your cooperation in this matter. I hate to put you under the gun and I apologize for my abruptness, but time is of the essence. I hope you understand my dilemma. I must add that you have unlimited authority to pirate any and all research people from competing companies to assist you in this project. If you require special machinery— go get it. If you believe that you should use containers to hold food ---go get them. If any competitor complains and moans about this, have them call my office. Do not concern yourself with the financing of this project. What we require is results."

And with that, Adam rose from his chair. The meeting, as far as he was concerned, was concluded. Jackson stopped him, "Dr. Andros, I know the pressures that you are under and we did not want to make light of your efforts. Zak Fellows explained your dilemma, we shall get back to you as soon as we can. We would hope that you consider us as part of your pay load."

Adam took a deep breath, exhaled slowly and gave his standard answer, "Gentlemen, right now, I don't know if I will be considered part of that pay load. That is way down the road. Thanks for coming under short notice."

Jackson and Abba nodded. Too much work had to be done by all sides.

Adam took a deep breath as the two visitors left his office; another part of the project would be worked on.

CHAPTER XI

The following week, Adam was at his desk trying to consolidate the timing of his subcontractors delivery of the various components of the ship. It was almost five when the phone in his outer office rang shrilly. It seemed louder than usual. After the second ring Jebba picked it up but immediately ran into his office, her face as Andros as a sheet, "Doc, you gotta pick this up. It's Eve, something terrible has happened."

Adam picked up his extension without any further explanation leaving Jebba standing by the doorway with tears rolling down her cheek. "God, Eve, what the hell is goin' on? Jebba is having a breakdown."

"I guess you haven't heard, but the President was shot an hour ago as he was coming out of a meeting. It's on the radio and people are screaming in the streets. It's awful."

"Is he alright?"

"What has been announced is that he took a bullet in his shoulder. From what his Chief of Staff reported just now, it's not life threatening, but it could have been. They caught the guy who did this but it's after the fact."

Adam held the receiver in his hand for a minutes without any words forthcoming. What could he say? Finally, "Do they know why he did this?"

"The preliminary report is that he blamed the President for the problems we are experiencing. There is much more to the story I suspect, but at least the President will be okay. I'll be home late tonight. Take some food from the freezer or stop in at a fast food spot. Hope I didn't scare Jebba too much. See you later."

Adam just held the receiver and watched Jebba standing against the threshold tears running down her face. "It's okay, Jebba, Frisca is okay. He was just wounded." Jebba burst into tears as she ran out of his office.

He could not say another word. What he had heard about conditions of the population have become a reality.

He immediately called the President's house. The phone was picked up before the second ring, "This is Zak Fellows, Chief of Staff, I have no news to report...."

Before Zak could continue, Adam butted in, "This is Adam, is the President okay? Can we continue with the project? Just give me the basics. My God, tell me something!"

"Good God, Adam, I've been hoping it would be you. I've been bombarded with questions from every newspaper reporter for the past two hours. Frisca is okay. He'll be wearing a sling for the next couple of months but fortunately the bullet just missed some vital areas. His arm will be stiff for maybe a year. His last words to me before being taken to the hospital was I should tell you full speed ahead on your project. However, there are two items that you should be aware of. One, be aware of a Senator Jacobs. If he gets any clue about your plans to send a space vehicle to another planet, he will be on your back requesting passage and authority to make those choices. Just play it cool with him. Secondly, keep Chad up to date with your progress. He will relate all of your progress to me."

#

The following morning, Adam was standing before the President's hospital bed. It was just eight, but he had to get the President's direct word on continuing the space ship program. Frisca removed a breathing tube from his nose, there was an IV drip attached to his right arm, "You're up early Dr. Andros, you must have either good news or bad. I haven't had my morning beverage so you better give me the good news first. The bad news is that my arm hurts like hell." He laughed weakly.

Adam, fully understanding the President's dilemma, just shook his head. "Mr. President, I realize that this may not be a good time, but I need to have your approval to go ahead with this program. I don't know where all this work will take us but there is a chance that we may be able to rescue a few hundred people. We have enlisted every capable engineer and scientist on the planet to work on this project. Their work is slow, as we had expected, but we do see some progress. I would be more comfortable if I got your okay directly from you."

Frisca tried to lift himself off the bed with no success, "Adam, I thought I told Zak, you are to go ahead with your program full speed. You have complete authority over this program...go." Frisca fell back on his hospital bed... exhausted. Adam got the mandate he was looking for!

CHAPTER XII

During the following weeks, Adam's phone rang continuously from his sub-contractors complaining they were not getting cooperation from their suppliers...'what were they to do?' and then on Tuesday after one ring, Jebba picked it up. She held her hand over the receiver as she whispered, "Dr. Andros, it's Senator Noah Jacobs. He claims that he is on the President's cabinet and would like a few words."

"Jetta," Adam immediately answered, "put him on, put him on."

"Yes, Senator, what can I do for you.?"

"Dr. Andros, I know how busy you are but could you spare me a hour for a drink this afternoon? There is a question that our subcommittees would like to resolve. How about twelve at that diner near your office?"

Not knowing what the Senator had in mind and wishing to maintain a good relationship with the administration, Adam agreed.

At five to twelve, Adam entered the drink shop and was waved over to a table in which Senator Jacobs stood, hand outstretched with an exuberant smile on his face. "Sit down, Dr. Andros, I've ordered you a drink so we can discuss matters of the day." Adam was impressed by Jacobs' take charge attitude.

After a couple of sips from their juice glasses and some small talk about the weather and people's reaction to it, Jacobs opened the conversation. "Adam, my committee has been receiving a number of large expense bills relative to the attempt to build a ship of some kind. This is perfectly acceptable as it has been approved by the the President. Considering the problems that you face this is perfectly acceptable to the legislators. However, I can see that since the work is moving along at such a rapid pace, you will require additional committees to get this project off the ground. I may be incorrect but I would believe that you will require a chairperson to determine who will go on this ship. We would believe that this would be the next order of business. Am I out of order with this comment? Is that thought on your list of priorities?"

After listening to Jacobs many useless words, Adam had to get to the point of this meeting. "Senator, we certainly appreciate your confidence in our project. We hope that it will be successful, but the project that we are working on is in the early stages of development and it is much to early to seek a chairperson for such a task. When the time comes, and it may be another year until we are up to that point, we can discuss its chairperson. Our engineers first have to determine if they can build a ship to meet all the needs of intergalactic travel. As I should have told you, Sir, that committee will be organized to make that decision as to who will be on the ship. I will try my best to keep removed from their selections. I assure you that I will remain completely neutral in their choices. The final decision who shall be on the voyage shall be determined by the President."

Jacobs refused to allow this subject to drop and so after another sip of his beverage he said what was on his mind, "Adam, I do not have to tell you, but I would consider myself capable to be the chairperson of that committee. If not chairperson, at least a member of that group. When that time comes, I suggest you tell that individual of my willingness and ability to serve. I will be a valuable member. Can I depend upon you?"

Trying to end this subject, Adam's response was quite curt, "Senator Jacobs, when the time comes, I will speak to the assigned chairperson."

Jacobs interrupted Adam with a bit of sarcasm, "Dr. Andros, excuse my interruption, but I have received information through my sources that you have already evaluated and considered a number of potential candidates, may I consider that information rumors."

Adam felt his short temper start to boil being interrogated like this, but trying to keep friends in the administration all he answered was, "Your rumors are just that, Senator, just talk. My sub-committee has interviewed a number of possible candidates and at this time all we have is a list of those who have been recommended to us. You, in fact, may be on that list. The appropriate person will get back to you when he or she believes you meet their needs." He quickly got off his chair, tossed a few bills on the table and was out the door before Jacobs could continue this discussion.

Adam went immediately back to his desk and ringing phones.

CHAPTER XIII

It was four weeks later that the President and Adam were enjoying breakfast in the President's Mansion. "This is a treat, Adam, being able to sit with you nose-to-nose without being hounded by my staff or political wolves. Since the shooting I've not been allowed to be by myself and have missed talking to you directly about our problem. Every time I leave the building, I am surrounded by military police or local guards. The summary of your progress is great and Asok's translations are fine, but I'd rather hear from you directly. But, first of all I wanted to treat you to the last glasses of my favorite juice. We are celebrating the last time we can have my favorite breakfast fruit drink. It's being taken off the market; the fruit will not grow in this cooler weather. I guess this was to be expected. I just thought it would have taken longer before the climate would have affected the crops. Life is difficult Adam, enjoy your last glass."

"Thanks for ruining my breakfast, Mr. President, but it's great to see you dressed and ready to join the real world. How's your shoulder by the way?"

"Still stiff as a board and I still need to take some meds to ease the pain, but you're not hear to to discuss my medical problems."

"You're right, Mr. President, let me get back to the project in which we are involved. Here's a ten minute summary of how things are progressing. With all the contractors and sub-contractors working seven days a week, twenty- four hours per day we are seeing some progress. Even they they still have a long way to go, especially with completing the space vehicle. They are close in discovering a unique metal composite that should give the ship the strength and durability that the engineers are looking for. Davis, tells me that after further testing they will be placing an order for shipment of that composite. If it has the properties that are needed we should have it by the end of the year. Then they have to add all the accessories. It's amazing how many nuts and bolts are required to furnish a space ship. Davis and his Engineering Group are proceeding slowly and surely, it's a start.

"Jonah's project is moving along slowly, but I have faith that he will discover an alloy combination that will give his batteries greater horse power and still be reduced in size."

Frisca took a long sip from his fruit juice glass, "Things look as if they are moving along, Adam, do you think it's about time for you to consider the worst part of the program...how many will go on the ship and who will they be. I would think you need some chairperson to coordinate that bit of business.

When will you interview for a committee chairperson? Would you consider taking on that position?"

"Mr. President, let's not even touch that subject. At this point in time I don't even know what the payload of the ship will be. Down the road, that committee will be making those choices. How they will choose those passengers, as of this date, I can't imagine. This is why I am giving careful thought as to who should head up that committee, call it a Ethical Committee, who will make those decisions. I really want to hold off for a couple of months an announcement of my choice but since you brought it up, to answer your question, I have done some preliminary screening for that position."

Frisca continued to press Adam as he asked, "So, who will be on the short list to be the chairperson or have you already made a final decision."

Adam ran his hands through his slight white beard and hair and over his tired face. He thought for a few seconds as his face showed the strain he had been under..."You're right, Sir, and I have been giving it a lot of thought. I've spent the last weeks contacting two dozen people asking their opinions and recommendations. Interesting, one name continually comes up. I believe that a Dr. Ani Shah can handle the job. Although I have not met her personally, her reviews are that she is an extremely well qualified lady. She was highly recommended by a number of executives in the academic world. She's the Chairperson of the Philosophy Department at Johnson University. I've studied her resume;

it's first class. Her being the Chair lady of a department of the most prestigious school on the planet doesn't hurt. I've spoken to the President of Johnson, James Robinson, and he maintains that she is an aggressive, self-directed lady who can make decisions and has exceptional administrative abilities. I just read her treatise on "Morality and Life.' The issues that she raised in her paper seem appropriate to our problem. I'm hoping that she would be willing to take on the job. I know if I were offered the position, I would turn it down. She better be a tough gal, this will not be easy." Adam exhaled, "I'm hoping that Shah will know how to run her show. From my research on her she is quite remarkable. With your permission, I plan to interview her within the next few months and offer her the job as Chair lady. I'd also would like to get her thoughts on how she would proceed. So please keep this information quiet. I hope that she is as capable as her associates claim she is. We have awhile to go before we tie down all the other loose ends and I ask her to take the job. She, in fact, may turn me down, but we'll take one problem at a time. We have to find out her toughness under fire."

"I understand, and she's a reasonable choice, Adam, but I would have thought you'd consider Robinson or Sam Samuels. I would believe with their backgrounds they both look capable. My God, Samuels is the ex-President and Robinson is the President of the best regarded college on the planet!"

"Your choices are good; in fact, both those men were two and three on my short list. I called their peers and business associates and the comments that I received were not that positive. One is egocentric and may have a problem working with others on his staff, while the other is too namby-pamby, and cannot make decisions. It would take him a year to make decisions. Right now I have other problems. Choosing a committee chairperson to decide who goes and who stays does not have my top priority. As you may know, our famous Senator Jacobs has thrown his hat in the ring and would like to be chairman of this committee. He was In fact, adamant about being a lead contender. I don't know what I'm going to do about him; and there are others who are casting their names in my direction."

"Did you consider Senator Jacobs after his veiled threat of how he could make things difficult for you?"

"How could he make things more difficult? He cannot bribe me, although he subtle tried. Money has ceased to become an issue. All the contractors are no longer asking for payments. What good is money these days? To be honest I think all these people are working just to keep busy. Wouldn't you?"

"I guess you're right."

"The bottom line, Mr. President, do I have your permission to go ahead and interview Shah?"

Frisca sipped his drink and briefly glanced at a pile of briefs that were on the table, "Adam, I gave you complete authority over this project. I have never disagreed with you and I will not disagree with you now. I know that you must have worked many hours choosing Dr. Shah. When the time comes go to it my friend. I appreciate you keeping me in the loop. I would never second guess you. If Shah is the candidate of choice, go with her. Funny, but I met her at a convention a couple of years ago and she sat at our dinner table; I was very impressed with her composure. She's a good choice. You'll keep me up to date after you interview her."

"Of course."

"She better be tough. I couldn't imagine what you would say if I asked Mrs. Frisca, Angi to be chair of that position. You know she has a couple of degrees in Child Physiology." Adam gave a weak smile. Frisca laughed, "That wouldn't be the worst choice. Now get out of here. Let me go to work."

CHAPTER XIV

The following week, Adam called the President's House, asking for the President. Zak Fellows, his Chief of Staff, answered the phone.

"Good to hear from you, Adam, we're hoping that you have good news."

"Zak, as usual, I have good news and bad news. I think the President should be brought up to date with this information. Can he spare me an hour later this week? How's he feeling?"

"He's still a little stiff. Fortunately the bullet went right through his left shoulder so he can use his right hand. Except for a shoulder sling he's doing okay, a little more grouchy than usual, but that's to be expected.

"We'll work you into his schedule at two on Wednesday. I know he's out of town on that day, but he does want to keep up-to-date with you."

Adam returned to his laboratory at one-thirty on Wednesday. All morning he had been visiting Ezra Davis of Davis Engineering. Davis was justifiably worried. First, he had to put up a double row of barbed wire around his plant. No one was allowed in or out. Not being able to leave the confines of the plant, his workers had to sleep on cots and in tents. They were not very happy. Second, a couple of hundred people were camping outside the perimeter of the fence hoping to get in. They, of course, had heard the rumor of a space ship that was being put together inside. They hoped, while some prayed, that they would be on the ship.

As Adam opened the door to his office, Jebba was standing at his desk, an annoyed look on her face. "Zak Fellows called at one, he was expecting you. The President flew back from his appointments to see you. I assume he was upset that you were not waiting for his call."

Without answering her, Adam quickly picked up his phone and dialed the President's office. The answer was immediate. "Dr. Andros, this is Zak Fellows, we were expecting you to be available immediately, where the hell are you? The President flew home especially to see you."

"Sorry, I was led to believe that the President would not be back in the city 'til much later. I had some extremely important meetings to attend. I will discuss these with you and the President. Please give him my apologies. When can I see the President?"

"As soon as you can, he will be waiting for you."

"I will be there in fifteen minutes."

Running out of his office, Adam yelled at Jebba, "I will be with the President, hold all my calls. I'll get back to them later this afternoon or this evening. Tell Eve what's going on." And with this he was gone.

Flagging down the passing bus, Adam entered the President's quarters in twelve minutes. Without any fanfare, he was asked to enter the large sitting room where the President discussed matters of state. Adam was taken aback by the presence not only of the President, Tomas Paul, Zak Fellows and Chad Asok but Noah Jacobs, sitting in a secluded corner with the smile of a cat that just ate the canary.

Quickly shaking the President's outstretched hand and Fellows and Asok, Adam quickly added, "I'm terribly sorry to delay this meeting, Mr. President, I misunderstood your arrival back in the city. I thought you would not be here 'til later today." He nodded at Jacobs, who returned his nod. He did not rise from his seat.

"Okay, Adam, let's get down to it. I understand from Asok and Zak that you have a number of things to tell us."

"That I do, Sir. But first, I am surprised that Senator Jacobs is at this meeting. The information that I shall discuss is extremely confidential and with due respect to the Senator, I do not think he should be privy to some of these disclosures."

Jumping to his feet, Jacobs said in a loud, nasty tone, "Who the hell do you think you are, you test-tube pusher. Four years ago you were an unknown in a second- rate lab in a small second-rate college. Now you think you're a God? If I wanted, I could cut off all your appropriations tomorrow. I belong here as well as these other gentlemen."

Still standing, Adam took a deep breath, exhaled it slowly, and said as quietly and slowly as he could, "Mr. President, almost five years ago, you gave me full authority over this misting dilemma. For the last years, my teams and I have worked exclusively on this problem. We have found the cause of the world's misting and subsequent cooling. We cannot prevent it. But we are working on a way where a few of our citizens may escape the calamity that will befall us. Please catch my words that this calamity will occur! It is not make-believe or made up. My monthly reports to your office has given you and Joda an up-to-date summary of our activity and progress. I believe that the Senator's comments are uncalled for and an apology is in order. If not, you will have my resignation on your desk tomorrow." Adam remained standing, his face flushed with anger, staring at the President.

President Frisca rose to his feet, hands in the air, "Gentlemen, gentlemen, we have all been working under a great deal of pressure and strain lately. Noah, I think some of your remarks were uncalled for, and I can understand Adam's sensitivity. The good Doctor is completely in charge of this difficult problem and is here in good faith with good news, we hope. Let him continue with his update. Please sit down, Adam, want a drink?" His attempt to defuse the situation was only partially successful.

Adam did not sit, "No thank you, Mr. President. I am waiting for an apology from the Senator and an answer as to why he is at this meeting." Adam's insides were boiling; he had not been that insulted in all his life.

The President sat in his over sized chair, adjusted the shirt sleeves under his jacket, and shifted some papers from side to side, "Adam, you and your people have been doing a magnificent job and I can understand your reluctance to disclose information. Let me say that Noah plays a vital part in this administration. And in that regard almost everything that concerns financing goes through his committee; understand? I respect his intelligence and his ability to help me run this government on a financial level. As for his unnecessary remarks, Noah, I believe you owe Adam an apology." He crossed his arms.

Noah Jacobs, Chair of the Appropriation Committee, answered with little enthusiasm, "Sorry, Dr. Andros, I was not aware that you did not know of my involvement with the President. I am sorry for my comments." He did not show any signs of repentance.

As if those few words closed the issue, with a large smile on his face, President Frisca said, "Okay, Adam, have a seat, let's get down to the issues. What do you have for us?"

Once again, Adam paused, but finally understanding that sometimes judgment takes the place of valor, sat and started. "After our last get together in which you and Zak gave me the current state of our country, I asked all of our contractors to speed up their work. And I'm happy to say some positive results have resulted. Within the past months we have been fortunate, and lucky, to have some good news. One, Dr. Eve has discovered a possible planet in our galaxy that she believes we can live in. She had been trying to locate this planet and now she's been fortunate to rediscover it. We believe it's years away, but at least we have a potential target that seems livable. Bottom line being— we may have a place to go. She has found that this planet moves on a elliptical curve which brings it closer, at times, to our planet. If we can catch one of those curves we may be able to save a great deal of time. We will be be closing in on one of those eclipses within six months. So you see time will be playing a factor in our progress."

"So the bottom line, Adam, is that we must move our tail off Zavre within six months? Adam, is this possible?"

"Mr. President, it'll be tight, but that is what we must shoot for."

"Okay, what other great news do you have."

"Second, Dr. Blanca's research group has developed an power energy package that will be able to get our space ship off this planet. Of course, his energy system depends on the size of our space ship and the number of its passengers. The maximum number of passengers that this propulsion system can tolerate is two hundred and fifty."

President Frisca raised his hand to interrupt Adam's additional words.

"Adam, let's stop right there. We were depending that your engineering people could build a vessel to contain five hundred passengers. I am aware of the implications that even that number will mean that we will be leaving a couple of million to their eventual death. But what happened to that original thought? Has your engineering people considered building multiple ships. This may be a little late to bring up this subject but why are they spending all their energies on one ship?"

"Mr. President, our main contractor, Davis Engineering, has experience in the construction of aircraft to hold three hundred passengers. They are only one of three engineering companies that can even build a vessel that size. For them to up-size and increase the capacity of that ship or to build an additional ship to hold five hundred is an impossible task. For Davis to go to even a larger ship, or another ship, would require additional material and new engineering studies involving wind and vibration analysis, something that would have taken an additional three or four years. Gentlemen, as I had just stated, we just don't have the time. Mr. President, our conversation with Ruben James last week only confirms the fact that if we are to meet our time requirements we have to speed up our program. On another subject, but still related I am sure that you are noticing a decrease in the temperature. It is becoming more and more obvious and will become more severe in a couple of years. The deciding factor was that the energy source developed by Dr. Blanca's people could, at the best, lift two hundred people and the payload off our planet. To paraphrase Dr. Blanca, every pound of weight we put on this ship will require a certain amount of energy to free it from gravity. The weight factor is even more critical."

Frisca stood up from his chair, walked around the room, his good hand in his pocket in deep thought. He was visibly upset. He picked up a paper-weight from his desk, read the inscription on its side and replaced it. "I thought, Adam, that one thousand passengers was a doable thing."

It was quiet in the room. Adam thought he heard Noah Jacobs breathing. "Sorry, Mr. President, that number is just not possible and I am aware of the implications that you mentioned. I, too, would have like to see us built a larger ship or two, but after months of discussion with all the various engineering firms on Zavre, Davis Engineering was the only contractor who even has the manufacturing ability and where-withal to construct half the size of a size space craft. It does not make us very happy, but we have to be realistic in our demands. In fact, Davis would like to see us considering one hundred passengers, but I convinced him that two hundred would be more acceptable. Ezra Davis is still pushing for one hundred passengers. I'm not happy with that number but he is the expert, so who knows.

"But, gentlemen, let me go on to another reason I asked for this meeting. The progress on the building and outfitting the space ship is moving along and we must, at this time, bring up a subject that perhaps affects us even more than the deciding of how many passengers we shall place on the ship.

"At a private meeting with the President, I explained that after much soul searching and investigations, I will be asking Dr. Ani Shah of Johnston University to chair an Ethical Committee. This committee will determine who shall be the passengers on this space ship. With the President's acceptance, I will approve those members to be on that committee. After she prepares such a list, I will show them to the President who will give them the final okay."

It was quiet in the room; someone started to drum his fingers off the wooden table. Then Senator Jacobs rose from his side chair. He responded with a look of arrogance and with a voice that showed his displeasure, "Dr. Andros I've heard rumors that you selected Dr. Shah for this Ethical Committee of yours, but I couldn't believe it. I was hoping to be asked to chair that committee. I offered my name to you some months ago with good intentions. With my experiences, I believe that I could handle that responsibility. Is it possible for you to withdraw that offer to Shah?" He looked at the President for approval and support.

Adam responded, "Senator, I know that you offered yourself as a candidate, but after much thought I believe that Dr. Ani Shah seems to have all the qualifications we were seeking. I have discussed her qualifications and background with the President and he agreed to my choice. She has graciously accepted that position and is now in the process of choosing her committee members. If you were not called for that position it was for valid reasons that I would not like to discuss at this time. As we speak, she is calling those prospective members for their acceptance. I am not sure that your name was on that list. If she feels you are qualified and have all the abilities she require, she will contact you."

Jacobs, obviously not happy with that answer, continued, "Abilities! What abilities does she have that I do not have? Dr. Andros I think you are making a grave mistake that will determine the lives of many of our citizens. I cannot believe that you will accept one person's opinion who should be on this ship."

"Please, Senator," Adam immediately answered, "You did not understand me. Shah will not make these decisions, her committee will do so."

For the first time, Dr. Chad Asok spoke, "Senator, first, if my hearing is correct, Dr. Andros is correct, Dr. Shah will not select the passengers. Her committee will select the appropriate group. Another group will be selected by the same committee. Second, I've had firsthand experience with Dr. Shah. She is the highly qualified person in the most highly respected school on the planet. She is a superb administrator who can run this committee with due diligence. I'm sure that Dr. Andros took all of that information into account before making his decision. I cannot disagree with his choice. It is an excellent one. Noah, I think you should back away from this. Let Adam and Shah do their unrewarding job."

Jacobs, not willing to give up his requests so readily looked at Frica, "Your thoughts, Mr. President?"

President Frisca stretched and cracked some knuckles on the fingers of his good arm. He tented his fingers, allowing him to gain a few seconds to consider his response, "Noah, the mark of a good executive is to appoint competent leaders and allow them to lead and listen to their opinions. I have supported Dr. Andros for over four years and his research and abilities are above reproach; I cannot argue with his choice of Chairman. I have also had the opportunity to meet Dr. Shah at some functions and I must say it would be difficult for me to veto Adam's choice. Adam, do you know how this committee will choose their two hundred passengers?"

"At this time, I do not have that answer. I am leaving all of that procedural stuff in her hands. I assure you she has the experience and ability to do so."

Not willing to let Adam get away, Jacobs added his final dig; "I assume you will tell Shah that I expect to be on that committee and I intend to play an active role."

"Of course, Senator, of course; if you are selected," Adam answered, as he looked at the President.

Jacobs look at Adam was not one of friendliness.

Attempting to leave the office Adam was stopped by the President's hand. "You know Adam, when I first took this job I thought my priorities would be unemployment, education and health issues. In retrospect, those would have been easy to solve and now one of our citizens takes a shot at me. What would have happened if he didn't miss? I wonder at times what the devil I got myself into."

Adam had to smile, "Mr. President, someone always has to get stuck with the tough jobs. Fate just decided that it must be you. How is your shoulder getting along?"

"It's still stiff and it's a pain when I try to sleep, but I can live with it. Thanks."

"How is Mrs. Frisca taking all of this?"

"How could she? She's no fool. She realizes that eventually a decision will have to be made who goes on this magic trip of yours. This thought is not making her a happy lady. I am sure that she is like thousands of mothers on the planet worrying about their families. Getting back to the business on hand however, arrange to see me for breakfast when you have pertinent news. Before these vultures," he motioned with his head, "get to me. I need an immediate update on your plans. Things are getting very up tight around here and I'm being pushed from one corner to the other by political forces. It seems that every Senator now has become my dearest friend and that I can push their name to be passengers. They cannot believe I have left all that good stuff for you. " He winked as if Adam understood the implications.

CHAPTER XV

The following month, the phone rang in Adam's office which Jetta immediately picked up, "Dr Alexia, it's the President's Chief of Staff, Zak Fellows. He wants to speak to you."

"Put him on," was the immediate response.

"Dr. Andros, is your phone secure?"

"Excuse me?"

"Dr. Andros, with the weather getting unseasonably cool and the President's words starting to sink in some of our congressional representatives realize what the only alternative may be. They are hoping to be put on a short list to join you on your adventure. Got my drift? They want to be kept in the loop. I was told that some of them are tapping into our phones to be kept up-to-date."

"Mr. Fellows, I understand your comment, but we are not nearly at that stage of preparation. It'll be months until we get to that point, but why did you call?"

"An Appropriation Committee of the Congress is meeting to discuss your request for unlimited funds for your project. They require your presence to discuss your financial needs and long term plans. But to be honest with you, Adam, I wouldn't be surprised if the question of travelers on your space ship is not brought up. Be prepared to be interrogated on this topic. Good luck, my friend."

"My God, Zak, this is just the early stages of our program. Are we going to let party politics get in the way of solving this awful problem? I was told by the President that I would have control over all finances, and money will not be an issue. Is this going to be an issue?"

"Adam, politics and money always get in the way of reality. We have to be pragmatic. There will always be people trying to pull their weight and seeking to get a step up. We have to live with them. Join the real world. Are you joining us?"

"I accept an invitation to this Committee on two conditions. One, I would like to appear with Dr. Esta and second, this meeting is to be closed to all radio, TV or outside publicity. The members of this committee must swear that they will not disclose any of my remarks to anyone. If the population was aware of what is occurring and its seriousness, I'm afraid that there may be greater panic and riots. I cannot be held responsible for that action."

There was a long quiet on the phone. Adam heard some whispering in the background, a couple of muffled heated words and then Zak got back on the phone," I will do the best I can."

"Mr. Fellows, with due respect, you have to do better than that, otherwise I'm a no-show."

This time the pause was much shorter, "Okay, Adam, you're on for Monday at ten. Bring your friend."

"Before you hang up, Zak, is the President aware of this call?"

"Although he thought it was a waste, he thought it was politically necessary."

All Adam was able to say to himself was, *"Damn* politics."

#

The following Monday, under the slightly misting sky that mirrored Adam's feelings, Adam and Eve drove in their two door, four seater *Scat,* to the Government building. That the car ran on batteries and could go one thousand miles before re-charging was due to the past development by Jonah Blanca. A heavily armed guard escorted them to a back door to an out of the way meeting room in the Capital Building. Adam immediately realized that it was prepared for an interrogation. He and Eve were to be seated facing a raised dias, already occupied by five Senators. There was a small placard before each Senator indicating his or her name and district represented. He held onto Eve's hand tightly, not that he required her help in these type of matters; he was well versed in the some-time belligerency and rudeness of these committees, but he needed her to calm him when the comments became too nasty and aggressive as they sometimes did. He tried not to be intimidated, but in reality how could he not be with five pair of hostile eyes staring down at him.

Chairman Noah Jacobs started the conversation with a remark, which caused the hair on the back of Adam's head to stand and his blood to boil, "I was not aware, Dr. Andros, that you and your assistant were romantically involved."

Eve leaned over and whispered in Adam's ear, "Play it cool, Adam, play it cool."

"Senator Jacobs, I was not aware that my personal life would be discussed here. Dr. Maros s not my assistant; she is my co-worker and one of the most brilliant minds in her field on the planet." Eve squeezed his thigh under the table to show her appreciation for his words. "Can we get to the topic of this meeting? I think that is more important to this committee than my private life."

Noah Jacobs sat back on his chair, a slight flush entering his face, "Sorry, Dr. Andros, you are perfectly correct, there are more important things to discuss.

Over the weekend we interviewed Zak Fellows and he has given us a summary of your comments with our President. Frankly, this committee cannot accept these totally negative reports. Our advisors indicate that the problem of global cooling is a temporary one or one that we can survive or better yet, live with. I'm going to ask the members of this committee to question your logic and rationale on your current thoughts on this matter. Before you and your select committees go off half-cocked spending billions of quatros on a project that may not have any value, the Congress and specifically the Appropriations Committee, want to know how valid your open-ended request is for money. Senator Zello, you have five minutes."

Before Zello could begin his interrogation, Adam commented, "Excuse me, gentlemen, besides questioning Fellows, did you speak to Dr. Asok? He would be the logical choice to obtain valid information. As you are aware, he is the President's technical adviser and was present at our meeting and receives my monthly summary of our activities..."

Senator Jacobs interrupted Adam as he was going to continue his line of thought. "Dr. Andros, we are well aware of Asok and his knowledge. We, in fact, also interviewed him. He was not very helpful, almost mimicking the remarks of our Chief of Staff. If we are going to give you carte blanche to spend on a non-existent emergency, how can we explain this to our constituents? Please allow us to follow our own protocol and routine."

Adam felt dampness under his arm and a wetness run down his back. Eve leaned over and whispered, "Just answer their stupid questions Adam, it won't take long. Be patient with these dummies."

For the next two hours Adam was bombarded with questions he had already discussed with the President, Fellows and Asok. Although the Senators asked a few more detailed questions, Adam's responses were exact and to the point and were the same answers he had previously given to the administration. Nothing that the Senators could ask went unanswered, much to the chagrin of the Senators who were seeking some flaw, some discrepancy in his research or in his line of thinking…none were forthcoming. Adam was prepared, he did not fumble with his words nor did he waver in his responses.

After the Senators had their day in the sun, Jacobs finally said, after taking a sip of water, "Okay, Dr. Andros, I believe you have answered all of our questions to the best of your ability. I have to admit you have come prepared."

"Senator, my group and other authorities in the field have been working on this and related problems for more than two years. We have attempted to resolve many of the problems you raised. Most are still pending and when they are resolved we will get back back to you and the committee in good order. As the President says,'we are doing the best we can.'"

With some sarcasm Jacobs responded, "I'm sure you are," as the committee shuffled some papers and put additional data on a screen.

Once again, Eve leaned over to whisper to Adam, "Have patience, Adam, have patience."

Jacobs ignored Eve's whispered comments, as he continued, "Allow this committee to now ask you a more pertinent question. If the results of this misting are so deleterious, you must be considering alternatives. Possibly a method to leave the planet? How large a space ship do you plan to build? Do you plan to build more than one? How many people will leave? Will you be the God to determine who will live and who will stay to die? I need not go on; I think you catch the intent of this group. To the best of your ability, what are your thoughts on this side of the issue?"

Adam's blood was boiling. He would have stood up and spoken his piece to these overblown ego maniacs but Eve once again whispered in his ear, "It's okay, Adam, tell them what you know."

Adam took a deep breath and exhaled slowly. This technique seemed to have relieved some of his tension. *Best of my ability.* "Gentlemen, you are placing the cart before the horse for me to discuss methods of leaving this planet, the size of the space ship, how many people it will hold and who they may be. The number of passengers the space ship may hold is strictly dependent upon the energy sources we can develop. Our engineering people are working on the construction of an additional ship. Obtaining the right quality metal covering is a major problem. I think that answers part of your questions.

"But, Senators getting back to the Senator's question, whether we take one thousand, five hundred or one hundred will only be determined by the size of the space vessel and the size of the space ship will be determined by the power needed to send it into space. Although your questions are appropriate, they are all premature. As I said before, speak to me in a few months. What is more critical now is that we receive all the financing and cooperation we need to continue the program. May I assume that you will see to that?"

"I'm sure we will, Dr. Andros, I'm sure we will, but you can see our position. I cannot go back to our constituents and say we will be spending billions of quatros on a project that may not have any chance of success. Furthermore," Jacobs continued, "we would like to be considered to be on the list for the passengers on the ship and your engineering people should strongly consider one thousand passengers rather than the lower numbers you mention."

"Senator Jacobs, the numbers that I mentioned should not be considered final. I just used them to indicate the possibilities involved reference our pay load. As I said previously, it's not up to me to determine the people involved nor the number."

"Not for you to say? Not up to you to say?" Jacobs was sounding hostile. "Who then would make that critical decision?"

Once again Adam had to take a deep breath to control himself, "To repeat myself, one, our Engineering Group and Ezra Davis of Davis Engineering will determine the number of people that this ship will hold, and that number will be determined by our energy capabilities.

"Your comment about my being a God to determine who goes and who stays is uncalled for and, in fact, quite insulting. At our previous meeting with the President, I mentioned that I was seriously considering a Dr Ani Shah as a chairperson for that committee. As of this date I have not spoken to her about the situation. The committee that she appoints will make the decisions who are the designated passengers. I do not intended to take part in those decisions.

Jacobs looked at his other committee members and grunted, as if he did not believe that comment, "We will be seeing you then, Dr. Andros. I believe this meeting is over. Thank you for your time." He rose and with the other four members gathered in a corner to further discuss some of Adam's responses.

As Adam and Eve were preparing to leave the room, Jacobs, who had pulled himself away from his colleagues, accosted them. "Adam, could you spare me a minute— alone? Something private."

"Senator, I assure you that everything you say or ask in Eve's presence is okay. Feel free to say what you want to say."

Jacobs finally said what was on his mind. Something that he had planed to bring up without the rest of his committee in attendance. "Dr. Andros, some time back, I suggested that you consider me to be on the group who chooses those citizens taking that voyage. Perhaps my comments were not strong enough, I would like to insist at this time that you, as Chairperson of this total project, insist that I be placed on this group. My being left off would not be a sign of friendship." Jacobs face was the the color of a cooked turnip. He had obviously lost control of himself.

If Eve were not holding Adam's suit jacket, he would have punched the Senator. But once again taking discretion for valor, he responded, "Senator, our first order of business is to secure the building of a space ship. If that is not accomplished within six months the selection of a Ethical Committee chairperson will be wasted. There are probably one hundred people who would fit into your category. Notwithstanding the fact that you may be chosen, I would leave this final decision to be determined down the road. We are not quite ready to make that decision."

"Adam, let me give you a bit of advice. In all my years in politics, I've discovered that there is always some wheeling and dealing goin' on. If you want the cooperation and all the appropriations you want, you ought to reconsider some of your priorities. If you would like your contractors to receive the funds on time and keep the project going without any stoppage or slow down, it would be wise to cooperate with my committee."

"Senator, there is a better than average chance that Eve and I may not be on board that vessel. We do not have any preconceived notion as to how this will all pan out. I realize how difficult this may be for you, but at this time, we're all in the same boat."

"Once again, Adam, let me repeat, you should consider it in your best interests that I be considered a member of that committee." He took a breath and then continued, "Life is not as perfect as you may believe it to be. If you play your cards right, I can make it easier for you."

Adam clenched his fist as Eve pushed him to the door. She answered, "Senator, we'll let you know how things are developing." And with that, she shoved Adam out the door as he muttered, "Son-of-a-bitch."

#

After an evening of arguing with Eve about how Adam's meeting with Noah Jacobs had gone, Adam was exhausted. Eve's comments suggested that he had given in too easily to the disgusting remarks by Jacobs and that he should have resigned. "Let some other idiot run the show," she screamed at him. When Adam screamed back, "And who do you suggest, Eve, I love you dearly and what you are saying is, as usual, correct, but I have to look at the bigger picture. We'll give Jacobs his day in the sun by putting him on the committee and we'll see what transpires. I'm sure the chairpersons I am considering can handle that big mouth."

Eve slammed the door of the bathroom as she proceeded to her bath.

Adam turned back to his screen. He was not happy with the water temperature charts that had been sent him in which he was comparing sea temperatures for the past fifty years. He viewed icebergs the size of glaciers floating down the ocean. The figures were not pleasant; the oceans had retreated from the coastlines almost ten feet.

A half hour later Eve exited her bath, the color of a pink rose, a large towel wrapped around her and fire in her eyes. “Adam, I can’t believe that you allowed them to dump on you like that. For the last three year, you’ve been working your tail off getting all the facts straight and coordinating all the possible information. Frisca gave you total responsibility on this problem and now that ass Jacobs wants in. Screw him.”

Eve put her drink down on the table and with a solemn, quiet voice, “Adam, this is a hellava time to discuss this project we got ourselves into. It’s been almost three years and my people are exhausted from all the frustrating results we have been getting. Our sky screening and analysis are interesting but nothing is forthcoming. It’s pretty impossible to see or hear anything in the universe when we are getting more and more covered by this fog that is surrounding us. I have people leaving every day because they see no results. They see no success.

“Adam, I do have faith in your plans and enthusiasm, but do you really believe that we have the ability to get off this planet. We haven’t spoken to Jonah in months and when we do all he says is.’we’re still working on a new idea.’ I’d wish his ideas would stop and something positive would develop. I’ve been told that he went out and hi-jacked the best engineers on Zavre. By now I would expected some results. When you told him that he was to go all out on the project, he was very enthusiastic. Unfortunately, as of now, and it's been almost an two years, he still does not have the prototype he requires. The solution to his problem may take additional years to resolve. Are we foolin' ourselves?"

CHAPTER XVI

As the months and seasons slid by in an alarming rate, it became obvious to even the nonbelievers that the misting condition was increasing. The editorial pages of the major newspapers were now filled with a dozen questions and suggestions, to which, unfortunately, the government could not give any positive answers. At the beginning of this project, the government had ordered all media not to discuss what was really occurring with the misting program. Although the editors complained bitterly about censorship, they soon realized that too much information would not be something of which the general population should be aware.

Adam called the Presidential house and asked for the President. Zak Fellows picked up the phone. "Hi Adam, the President is busy trying to get the militia to put down some riots and insurrections on the other side of the planet. Things are getting pretty tight and chaotic. Is there anything I can tell him?"

"We think we will have to blast off in four months. At least, that is our tentative date. We have to get this goin'.

Speak to the President. Can he suggest something that won't cause a revolution?"

"The number of suicides has gone up dramatically over the past month", Frisca started the conversation. "To be honest, I cannot fault them for doing what they're doing. And there is nothing I can do to ease my country's pain. You are aware of the riots and looting that are occurring on the other side of the planet?"

Two days later, Adam, as instructed, was at the President's private eating quarters at seven eating a hot bun and sipping some juice while giving his update on the current progress of the space ship. The weather was noticeably cooler. It was not uncommon to see the population now dressed in coats, jackets, hats and gloves although according to the calendar it was late spring. President Frisca, who would normally appear in a freshly pressed suit and tie to match, would now join him in a sport shirt, heavy sweater, unshaven. The pressure of his responsibility was definitely affecting him.

"Adam," have you read the tabloids recently?"

"No Sir, I haven't read anything in the papers nor have I seen anything on TV. I just know what's happening in the city. It's not very pleasant."

"We've been trying to keep this type of news out of the media, but once in awhile some wise reporter leaks the story. This was a delicate matter that was discussed at a Cabinet meeting. The census was to keep the news off the airways and papers. All it would achieve would be additional mayhem. Half of our world is under martial law already. We live in difficult times, Adam; you have to get this space ship ready to go before there is complete insanity. I do not think you realize the extent of the cooling situation. Let me show you a picture of what the river looks like that flowed by the capital. It used to be a nice free flowing stream; now it is a frozen mess."

Taken from www.glacierguides.com

"I realize what you are saying and are preparing for that, Mr. President; we have increased security where we are assembling the space ships. Ezra Davis, CEO of Davis Engineering, has already told me of some nasty incidents. We are expecting the first delivery of food within the next few days. I hope their trucks can get into the assembly plant. The new batteries are being installed as we speak. We may need some militia to patrol the site. You're right, Sir, things are liable to get violent."

The President took a deep breath as if he were counting his words, "Adam, do you think that my family would have a chance to be selected to leave Zavre? I'm not talking about myself and my wife, but I have two sons and their families. I wouldn't like to have my family tree left on this dead planet. Does this committee of Shah's have any criteria of who to select for this trip? You have any thoughts on this?"

"Mr. President, I don't know if I and Eve will be selected. I do know that Shah has basic requirements for the passengers. Age, experiences, ability to live in a strange environment are just a few that I am aware of. I'm afraid we'll all have to wait. I can tell you this; I'd hate to be on that committee to make those decisions. Is there anything else, Sir?"

"You know it is quite amazing, Adam, a member of our Congress called the other day and asked where had all the water gone. He owned a yacht, and previously his boat would pull right up to his dock. The ocean now is a hundred feet from his docks. When he asked, 'Where is the water,' I had trouble convincing him that the water was gone into making ice sheets and glaciers. I think he thought I was crazy. A final blow to me happened yesterday when one of our top marine biologist give me a summary of the reduction in coral a major factor in fish growth. Go know?"

Adam had to smile, "I guess it takes the realities of life to convince some people we were not fooling with our findings. Is there anything else, Mr. President?"

The President's response was final; he just waved Adam goodbye as he left the table.

CHAPTER XVII

A month later after receiving some very promising results from Ruben James and then from Jonah, Adam realized that it was time to take the next step; and make the call that ultimately would effect the world of Zavre. "Jetta, please place a call to Dr. Ani Shah, she's a Professor at the University and should be in our directory."

"Is she going to be the chairperson of your special committee? Dr. Adam."

"Jetta, just make the call."

In ten seconds the phone rang on Adam's desk. He picked it up before the second ring, "Hi, Dr. Shah, this is Adam Andros.." Before he could utter another word, Ani Shah interrupted, "Dr. Adam, you need not introduce yourself to me and the reason for your call, my only question is what took you so long?"

Adam sat back on his chair and laughed. He had been alerted to Shah's aggressiveness but this was a little unexpected. Wow!

"Ani, you seem to have beaten me to the punch and the only thing I can say is when can you be in my office? At that time all questions will be answered."

"Now you're talking, Adam, I hope I can call you Adam, but I can be at your office by nine next Monday. I have some appointments to cancel. Soon enough?"

"It's a plan, Ani, see you then. We will be seeing a lot of each other down the road and formality will only get in the way. Besides, you out diploma me. They laughed as Adam hung up the receiver.

#

At eight-thirty the following Monday, after seeing the President for an up-date on their current activities, Adam told the President that he planned to have a meeting with Ani Shah later that morning. All Frisca said was, "Good luck, you may need it. Over the weekend I reviewed her credentials... she's a tough cookie and a great choice." Adam just shrugged his shoulders and answered, "Someone gotta do it."

Back in his office, Adam went back to reviewing his e-mails, faxes and answered two phone calls: one was from Davis Engineering telling him that things were moving along and our transport people put an additional hundred drivers on duty so they wouldn't delay getting transport to move the inner shields to the manufacturing site. His steel manufacturing sub-contractor added another sheet rolling system. If it is the quality metal we require, we will be happy. His sub-contractor put guards on all the trucks. This probably will speed up the installation by a couple of months.

"Jettta, I'm expecting a visit from Dr. Ani Shah at nine. I believe this meeting will be long and involved and obviously very important. From my research on this lady she's a tough arbitrator."

"With that intro, I hope she meets your needs, Dr. Andros, Jetta replied. "From what her responsibilities will be, she'll need a strong backbone."

At a few minutes after nine there was a short rap on the door of Adam's office. Jetta glanced at her watch and thought to herself, *well she sure is on time.* As the door opened, Jetta took a deep breathe as before her stood Dr. Ani Shah. Within five seconds, Jetta analyzed the person, who appeared to be in her late fifties, was going to determine the lives of of millions of Zavre's population. At perhaps five foot six, in low heels, she made an imposing figure. She sported short auburn hair that reached her shoulders in a page boy style that covered her forehead. But it was her eyes that grabbed Jetta. They were a deep blue that seemed to analyze the room and her in a flash. "I'm here to see Dr. Andros, he should be expecting me."

"Yes he is, Dr. Shah. Would you like something to drink?"

"Yes, thank you, but we'll see how much Adam has to say to me," she laughed. A slight throaty chuckle that tried to hide a voice that Jetta knew immediately would command attention.

Adam had opened his office door, by this time, and said, "Ani, please come in and take any chair that suits you and we can get down to the business and problems of the time. I'm afraid that some of the news you may hear may not be of your liking, but that's what we have to live with."

Ani Shah entered the office with an air of confidence that would have made a theater actress proud, and sat down in a chair that faced his desk, crossed her legs at the ankles and started her words before Adam could even sit down. Ani looked twenty years younger than Adam knew she was. She was dressed in the best of current fashion, hair perfectly in place and make-up selected to show her better facial features, "How are you this morning, Adam, ready to do battle?"

"Gee, I hope not, Ani. I had a battle all week with my girl friend and one of the top-ranked Senators. I hope our get together will be a simple event. But first things first: pull up a chair and can I get you a drink?"

"I'm fine, Adam," Ani answered, as she moved a chair closer to Adam's desk, "I'm sure you have things to tell me, go to it. You know, Adam, you never answered my initial question. It is still on the table?"

"And what is that Ani? I have a lot of question thrown at me? Most I ignore as I am not smart enough to know all the answers," he responded, smiling.

"You're a funny guy, Adam, but my question is still there. As soon as I heard the President's speech, I knew that down the road someone would have to be available to make some terrible choices. I knew I could be that person. Where have you been for almost four years. I've been waiting for your call."

"Ani, let's get that bit of protocol out of the way immediately. There were more important items for us to consider before calling you. We had to first determine if we had the capability to build a space ship to get people off the planet. If we couldn't do that your work would be unnecessary. But it seems that we have passed that hurdle and we are a step further down the road and you're next in line. I hope that brief answer answers your question. More important, let me give you the current state on the building of the space ship. As of this date this ship is designed to hold two hundred people. Can you envision how you will choose them? That is the basic question on the table that you and your committee members must resolve."

"Adam, I can see where you're coming from, and I appreciate your heads-up. By your call, I assume you are offering me the position of chairman of the committee?"

"Ani, you cannot refuse this offer."

"Well, let me then ask this question? I hope that I will not be a committee of one to choose those individuals to make this possible trip of yours?"

"No, no, Ani, I'm afraid you jumped the gun. I believe it would be better if you form a special committee, lets' call it, at this time, an Ethical Committee, who will make those decisions. The issue on the table now is who will be on that committee. Let me give you my starting list of those I would consider to be the ten members. I believe that ten would be a reasonable number." Adam slid a piece of note book paper across the desk.

"Consider this just a starting list. After you review these people qualifications, you may add to or eliminate any person you feel not satisfactory. A final list will have to be approved by President Frisca."

Shah finished her iced drink, "Okay, may I assume that you will be speaking to others about my appointment? Does anyone know who is on this list, or have you disclosed to anyone that you have offered me this job?"

"I'm in a dilemma, the only one who has any such knowledge would be the President and Senator Noah Jacobs. Jacobs quizzed me as to the make-up of the list. He came on rather strong asking to be chairman or at least being on the committee. I did not promise him anything, but expect to hear from him as soon as he discovers that I chose you as the leader. I hope it does not compromise your position."

"I think I can handle the situation okay, but more important, at least for me, how soon do you want this committee to be in place?"

"How about a month," answered Adam. *He prayed it would be sooner.*

#

Ani stayed in her office almost to eleven the next two weeks. She made almost three dozen calls to various friends and colleagues who she thought could give her advice as to how she should handle this delicate job. She had lunches and dinners with executive businessmen, scientists, doctors, religious leaders, educators some of whom she had not known for years. Everyone gave her their opinion until she felt her head ws going to explode.

She made an additional dozen calls to some of those reluctant members who were undecided whether to take on the responsibility. Six, who had initially agreed to be a committee member, backed off, stating that they did not have the temperament to pick and choose who shall leave Zavre. A number refused the assignment off-hand. A few even hung up on her. They could not conceive of themselves making such critical decisions. A few with strong religious beliefs did not want to play God to the rest of the world. Those who did say they were willing to accept the responsibility were checked out by additional calls to their peers and co-workers. Very often, the remarks that came back were not favorable and those candidates had to be eliminated. Calls came from Noah

Jacobs, once again giving his experience and ability to be in the group, but then adding that he still believed he would be capable of moderating the committee.

After further discussion, Ani realized that additional calls would have to be made and fortunately after an exhausting four days of calling her volunteers, she secured her eleven names.

It took almost a week for Ani to finally put together ten capable members of various Zavre's savants who she felt had the strengths and intelligence she needed. The following morning, Ani made an appointment to see Adam. In her purse was a list of citizens of Zevre who she hoped would take on the horrible task placed in front of them. Adam was on the phone with one of the engineers discussing how to handle waste products on the ship. Finally, he put down the phone and Ani slid over his desk a typed piece of paper that she had removed from her over- sized purse, "This is my list that I have prepared after our meeting. Sorry it took so long,but it was a horrible job almost begging for people to volunteer for this awful responsibility. I wanted to show you my ten choices for the committee. I'd appreciate your thoughts. These guys are going to decide who will be on the committee who will decide on life and death decisions on a lot of people. I hope you and the President will agree..."

Adam interrupted, "Yes, I'm sure that your names will be acceptable." He glanced briefly over Ani's names. Except for four conflicting names, almost all the names were those that he had considered. Robinson and Samuels had been included. "I'm glad to see you have included a few women at least, to balance a woman's views and thinking. I fully agree with your list of names, but I just about promised Jacobs a position on this committee, although he probably doesn't deserve it. Unfortunately, he has some clout with the President and to keep peace in the Administration, I was forced to say that you would consider him. Maybe you can include Senator Jacobs? It would make life easier for me. He is one big pain in the butt, but like everything else in this world politics plays an important and sometimes sickening role. I apologize for using my authority to suggest this ass. If you disagree with me, I can fight this out with Jacobs and the President; I just hate to. I'm sorry."

"You don't have to apologize, Adam. It's amazing, I received a call from the Senator over the weekend threatening me if I did not include him. Can you imagine? He said something to the effect that if I didn't give in to him he would have me fired from my position in the University. Fired from what, the country may be gone in ten years. His bullying techniques caused me to leave him off my initial list of ten person list I prepared. Sorry, if I jumped the gun but I knew eventually someone would have to prepare a list of those to be considered as passengers."

"I wouldn't believe that Jacobs would pull a stunt like that, but you never know with him. I suggest that you keep a tight rein on him during the committee meetings."

"Thanks for the notice, Adam, I will try to keep him under control."

Adam poured himself a glass of juice, loosened his shirt collar and after a deep breath started the discussion again. He felt this would be the tough part. "Okay, if you can live with that pretentious moron, we can move along."

"No major problem, Adam, let's get to the good stuff."

"Not so fast, not so fast, Ani. I still have to get Frisca's approval, which may take some time."

"Adam, I thought you had top priority on this subject. Frisca should be waiting with open arms for this info."

"You're right, but I'd be much happier if I got his approval of our select list, but more of that later. Fortunately, the President has given me the green light as to whom I can choose for all my projects. He has given me the okay for this one. I mentioned your name and your pedigree and he accepted you as Chairperson."

"Adam, I appreciate his confidence in me. I've been put in awkward situations before and so far have survived and as you have discovered someone has to do it. At my age I think I've got a tough skin. Let me start off by asking if the two hundred passenger figure is written in stone? Let's get down to more important issues: one, what would you suggest on the division or the choice of the people to be picked for this ride?"

"That's a tough question, but as of right now, we are trying to build a ship that will hold two hundred passengers. I sincerely doubt that that number will increase, unfortunately it may decrease. Please be aware that this number is secret and should not be disclosed to anyone and especially to your potential committee members until the time is right."

"Should I then consider that my group will have to choose two hundred residents?"

"Sorry, Ani, but that is exactly the question I wish you can help me answer. My initial thought would be if we can selectively choose one hundred talented residents and then, by lottery, choose the rest. How does that plan work with you."

"Lottery? That's' an interesting thought. You know Adam, anything we suggest will bring on a wave of dissent. It could even bring on a wave of violence, riots, anarchy…To answer your question, I guess I can live with an even split. I couldn't argue with that division. I'll bring up that possibility to my committee and see if it flies, I can see that this approach will cause some major problem. But now to more vital question: how will my group decide who the appropriate people are?"

Ani turned the ring on her right hand a number of circles as she thought out her response. "Adam, that's another tough question for me to answer off the top of my head. Give me a couple of days to consider some choices. Do you have any other thoughts?"

Ani looked about the room, for the first time noticing the pictures of past award winning scientists on the wall, and noted that although it was early in the morning, the haze covering the sun made it appear as if it were mid-afternoon. She pursed her lips, examined her nails and then looked with soulful eyes at Adam, "you know anything we recommend can cause a revolution!"

Before Ani could continue, Adam interrupted, "Ani, don't you think I thought about this before I asked you to head the committee? Of course we'll have problems; of course we'll have riots. We're going to have to live with all this. I hope the President is aware of these consequences and gives us protection. We surely don't need additional riots as what happened a couple of weeks ago. That would be disastrous."

"That is the rub, Ani. That is going to cause the trouble. Plan to call a meeting of your committee as early as you can. I'm sure that a lot of names will be thrown into the hat and blood will be spilled on the floor. I'm using that expression as a metaphor, you realize."

"I certainly hope so."

"Think of a method in which the leading authorities in survival techniques can be chosen. Include men and women who are leaders in the fields of construction, farming, conservation, administration and perhaps building. It should include some medical people. Of major importance would be those of a certain age group as well as those who you hoped were mentally stable. They could be stuck in a space voyage for five, perhaps ten years. Do you see from where I am coming, Ani?"

"I see where you are coming from and I think your first suggestion is not the worst in the world.

"Okay, Ani, what brilliant idea do you have that won't cause a revolution?"

"After a quick thought, I think your suggestion is not a bad one. The first group could be chosen by their experiences, their age, and their willingness to work together. The second group by lottery. They will still require the basic knowledge of surviving in a wilderness, but at least they came from the general population. It surely would be more democratic. I think I could sell that suggestion. I'm sure the committee will think of a half dozen other ways to choose. We would still have to take into account their ability to live in a hostile, strange world, but those individuals would be hand picked for those qualities."

Taking the last sip from his drink, Adam responded, "I will condense our lists of suggested committee members and show them to Frisca. I'm sure he'll okay our lists. I will try to get you the approval of the President as soon as possible. Once that is done, please expedite your meeting; this is most important. Move your group to some decision very quickly. Time is of the essence and we may have to leave within the next few months."

"As soon as I get the go-ahead from you, I will convene my group."

"That's fine with me. By the way, how are your classes going?"

"What classes, there are no more students in the school. They see no future. Why would they attend lectures on ethics and morality? The world has collapsed around them."

Adam sighed and shook his head in agreement, he knew that she was right, "Get moving on this, Ani, we are running out of time. Excuse me for cutting this short, but that call was from my engineering people and the food people. I do not want to miss their current status. I hope what they tell me is good news."

"I'll do my best, Adam. I see our group will be running long, long hours to chose our passengers. I expect that a number of people who we recommend will back down. They will not want the responsibility and I could not disagree with them. But let's see how it goes. I'll get back to you to tie up all loose ends. Is that okay with you?"

"Of course, please do your best with Jacobs. He can be one big pain."

With a grunt, Adam lifted himself off his chair, threw a large folder on his desk and said, "this is just a few of the items I must attend to today." He shrugged his shoulder's frustrated. Ani sipped the remainder of her drink while reviewing the list of names that Adam had handed her. She smiled inwardly realizing that Adam's list, with few exceptions, was almost a duplicate of hers.

Adam picked up his phone to see what his contractors wanted. The meeting, he thought, with Ani, went off better than he thought.

CHAPTER XVIII

Jebba put her head into his office, "You had four calls when you were with Dr. Shah. One was from your food producer, the other from your airplane builder. Jonah also wanted to drop a few words to you. They sound as if they have something important to say. The third was from our President. What shall I tell them?"

"I'll get back to them within the hour. The President's call had priority." Perhaps he was going to say something about his call to Davis.

"Adam, are you available later this morning? The President would like to have a word with you. He wants to bring you up to date on the status of Zavre.

"Zak, I hate to turn down the President's offer, but I have a critical meeting with Abba Able of Corporation Drug to discuss the space ship food supply and requirement schedule. Please give my deepest regrets but I think this meeting deserves my complete attention. Could we make it later in the day?"

“I’ll relay your message and thoughts to the President. I’ll get back to you within the hour. Our President is going crazy with suggestions and advice about your project from everyone on the planet who took a class in archaeology. It’s a miracle he hasn’t had a breakdown. He’s aged thirty years since he came out with the news.”

Fifteen minutes later the phone rang in Andros’s office. This time Jebba picked it up and after a few words, she yelled into Adam’s office, “If there’s no problem, the President will see you at four—be on time.”

#

As per Adam’s routine, he checked his top people every day to hear of any good or bad news. Their calls were usually negative but Adam hoped eventually that these calls would show some degree of progress.

Adam called Abba Able at Corporation Drugs. “Morning, Abba, how ya doing on my food supplements? Tell me something positive. Things are moving along on my end and I need some good news from you; a delivery date would not hurt.”

“Adam, you’re busting me. Yesterday I saw the first experimental filling machines that we made that would hold all the nutrients that our doctors said would be required. It is slightly larger than we would like, but we think it would be acceptable. We are trying to make it smaller. We will need another couple of months to finalize the formula and get the production people on board. They propose if the initial machine is not feasible, they will go the liquid nutrient route. The good news, Adam, is that the work we've been doing with the liquid nutrient seems the way to go. Unfortunately, that system would take up much more space than the tablets so we can't be dependent completely on that system. We have some problems with keeping the liquid mold free. It's a problem in itself. Our nutritional people think this may not be the way to go, but it's something to keep on the back burner."

"If it's a way out, Abba that may be the final solution. You're pill concepts sounded like the answer but after reconsidering the need for special presses and pill sizes, the liquid supplement may be the answer."

"Should I send to your lab a dozen of the first examples of the liquid system?"

"Unnecessary. By now you know the criteria. Try to make the food supply the one that is the easiest to produce in the quantity we will require. We'll give your people an additional month to get that moving. How about that for generosity?"

"Adam, you are overly kind. One thing however, if you're using these liquid supplements, you're going to require a fair amount of water or fluids to digest them. I hope you have planned to have enough water on board."

"Our resident doctor mentioned it to us. We also have to include trace amounts of calcium or potassium supplements. We have to consider something for motion sickness, bone loss as well as nutritional goodies. Even if we add trace amounts, everything we add increases the size. Our research people have been working overtime for the past year and they are getting discouraged. Besides that, my two best technicians left. Why, you're asking? they realize that they are not going to escape the events that will happen down the road. They're pragmatic. What can I tell them?"

"I understand your problems, Abba, and I wish I could give you some advice, but I'm afraid I have a host of my own. Tell them what I tell my staff,' try to stick with the program.' Do the best you can. Thanks for the heads up, our logistical man has already reminded us of our special needs. You guys are doing a fantastic job. Please tell Jackson that I'll be sending him a case of wine to show my appreciation..

He hung up. At least this part of the puzzle is showing progress.

#

With a bright, cherry voice, Adam returned Ezra's call. "How's my best engineer goin'. I thought I saw your ship fly over the President's mansion earlier today"?

"Don't be a comedian, Adam, we still need another two or three months to get our ship in flying condition. I'm waiting for a delivery of sixteen of Jonah's special batteries. I did not call you to exchange one-liners."

Adam interrupted, "Okay, Ezra what problems are you having excluding deliveries and manpower. We discussed those issues last week."

"I guess then you hadn't heard that Frisca called me earlier this morning. He was really upset screaming over the phone that he cannot accept a delivery of one ship to carry two-hundred passengers. Why I don't use the planes that was currently on the delivery line. He was so mad that I believe he threw the phone against the wall."

My God, Ezra, that's not like Frisca, he is usually an easy goin' guy. What could have upset him?"

"I guess when I told him that we have already invested a ton of money into those two ships, Chad Asok picked up the phone and just said, 'forget about the costs. The government will pick up all expenses.'

"Adam, I think you are to receive three ships carrying a total of seven-hundred fifty passengers. How you decide who goes and who stays should be an interesting exercise."

"Ezra, is there any possibility that you cannot met your deadline? If you have to convert those two additional ships will you require additional technical support?"

"Of course. Asok and Frisca do not realize that we would require additional made-to-order ceramic heat shields, lucite film. plexiglass and a dozen additional pieces. This would delay the project more than they realize. The installation of the booster rockets is also causing a problem. Your buddy Jonah's batteries are just now being delivered and installed. We're working around the clock with a depleted staff. On a positive note, we are expecting our first shipment of a lightweight aluminum steel alloy in a month. This will be used in the interior of the ship. Our engineers have ruled out the possibility of a two stage rocket system. It would be too involved from their current experience. Davis was hopeful that his engineers would be able to frame out the space ship within three months. It would take an additional six months to install all the electrical and navigational equipment. They were aiming to modify the interior of the airplane cabin to hold the two hundred passengers, a number that he felt would be acceptable for a lift-off condition. We will now have to adjust our time schedule to met the lift-off requirements. Thanks a lot.

"Adam, I trust you're aware that those people on this proposed trip should be instructed on how to live in outer space. Plan to give them a short course in weightlessness and how it could affect them."

"Thanks, Ezra, I hadn't thought of that but I'll include that in my plans after we choose those passengers. How long should that instruction take?"

"I think that five days should be adequate. On another matter, every day we've been losing some of our best engineers. They just don't want to work anymore. They see no reason for it. Some have even done themselves in with their families.

It's terribly depressing, but I thought you should be aware of this."

There was a long pause on the phone; finally Davis returned with an exasperated sigh, "Do not expect any luxuries on this trip. Adam. I can tell you this ship of yours is becoming a hotel. I can imagine all the pushes and pulls you are getting from all sides and I understand. You know I am losing more and more workers every day no matter what I offer them. They claim, 'What the hell are we goin' to do with the money."

"Ezra, I just wanted to remind you that we will require an extra amount of water on the vessel. I hope your logistical man has included that weight calculation into the final weight of the ship."

"Adam, we got the water requirements under control, but you're killing us. Your man, Blanca, called me some time ago giving me his parameters for the weight of the ship. Knowing the weight requirements, we've cut the interiors down in size and we've reduced the seat size to a minimum." There was a long pause on the phone; finally Davis returned with an exasperated sigh. Blanca also mentioned the need for a enlarged air conditioning system to compensate for the re-entry temperature that you will be experiencing. Thank God, that was a part of the original designs. Don't you have any kind words for me?"

"Ezra, before you hang up, I have another request. For this I may have a little bit of flexibility. Do you believe that you can reduce the weight of the ship…even fifty thousand pounds would be a help. We may need it to compensate for any additional people we have to put on board."

"You must be pulling my chain. Adam, what am I goin' to do with you? Okay, the bottom line is, how much weight should we try to remove?"

"My authority says fifty thousand pounds would be very helpful; more if you can do it."

"To this black comment, all Adam could say, with a heavy heart, "I'll speak to Jonah, maybe he has some brilliant ideas."

#

Adam put on his agenda the need to address a schooling program to instruct those chosen to be members of the ship. Could they live in an atmosphere of weightlessness for months or years on end? Could they manage the rigors of intra-galactic travel? Could they survive on the enhanced fluids they were being offered instead of real food? What type of training and exposure could Ezra Davis give them? How would it affect them physically…mentally? Davis suggested five days; how could that be fitted into their schedule?

The rest of the afternoon was equally exhausting and frustrating, Fellows spoke to him for a half hour telling him of the unrest in the city. He had to remind Zak that his plants needed to be protected from unruly crowds to allow his workers to get into the plants. All Fellows answered was, "I'll do my best."

Noah Jacobs called to say he had a fax from a reporter that an oceanographer informed him that the ocean temperature had shown a average decline of two degrees in the past six months. The reporter commented that his people felt that the temperature decline was increasing more than they've been told by the Government. Adam's heart dropped. He was aware of this decrease in temperature but its release to the public could only cause further unrest and problems among the population. They would have to work harder...and faster.

#

Adam showed up at the President's quarters at five to four. Abba Able had called back at two with terrific news. An additional automatic filling machine was being constructed to fill the plastic containers. It should be ready for delivery in two weeks. Able had discovered a small candy company on the other side of the city who filled plastic bags with chocolate bars. They will immediately start to fill those bags with food supplements. This news lifted Adam's spirit. *Maybe we are on our way,* he thought.

Adam was immediately shown into the President's sitting room where Zak Fellows was seated with a look of death on his face. Zak, appeared haggard and worn and looked as if he had aged twenty years since he was first introduced to Adam five years before. "Adam," Zak continued, "living in the Capitol, you cannot be aware of what is occurring in the outside cities. The world has completely changed since the President's speech on the misting situation a couple of years ago. There is chaos everywhere. Anarchy is the rule of the day. Police intervention is non-existent. Are you aware that people are now concerned with only day to day satisfaction? They want instant gratification. — why, you may ask, they may not be here tomorrow. All the banks have closed. Why or what should they save for? To whom should they loan money?"

Without further fanfare, Zak started the meeting, "Sorry, but the President and Tomas Paul are on his way here and will probably be a couple of minutes late, but I know he wants to see you. Let me start instead with some information for you. He has filled me in to the state of the nation. You should realize what is occurring in our small towns and cities due to this cooling situation."

"Adam, as we speak, the President is completing his speech about our mutual problem. He's trying to pacify some of the people from rioting and looting. In some small towns there is already mass hysteria with people burning their homes and committing mutual suicides. However, I know he would not want to delay your report. Adam, I could go on and on describing what is happening to our society. It is collapsing as I speak. I hope you do not think that I am exaggerating what I'm telling you, but I swear it's the truth. I do not know how far along your project is progressing, but you must speed up the work before we destroy ourselves completely and that space ship of yours just becomes a relic lying on the side of the road under ten feet of ice.."

With those words, President Frisca and Tomas ran into the room looking frustrated and disheveled, threw their jackets on a vacant chair, grabbed a glass of juice, left on the table, and joined the conversation. "Sorry I'm late, Adam, but I am aware of your activities. Chad Asok summarized your progress. I hope that Zak gave you a brief summary of what's goin' on outside the Capitol. I just spent the last few days traveling about and the situation is chaotic. Besides that my back is killing me from standing for hours making speeches. Some days I can barely move. But getting back to where I've been and seen on our planet...you must speed up the program."

Adam thought for a full minute, *what could he reply?* "Mr. President, Zak, Tomas, I am sure what you are saying is true. In fact some of my contractors are complaining that they are losing workers almost daily. But, please believe me, those that remain are orking twenty-four hours a day, seven days a week; equally their suppliers. Just this afternoon, Abba Able, our food supplier just reported completing the building of a special filling device to fill our food supply. It will still take almost two months to fill all the necessary containers. Fortunately, the manufacture of the liquid supplies are moving ahead of schedule. The development and production of the heat shields and booster rockets took almost two years and they are just now being installed and my story goes on. Our ship builder has just told us that the ship is progressing nicely and should be completed within a few months. I fully understand your concerns and we will try once more to expedite the program.

With that said, it probably will still take four months to say, "we have a go!"

Frisca looked over at his two visitors with mournful eyes, "Adam, I should tell you that I called Ezra Davis this morning. I guess I was having a bad day and Angi was getting on my case. Anyway, I came on strong to Davis and I told him to use his almost completed two ships for space ships. He was not very happy with that thought. He must re-engineer a great deal of the ship which was almost complete as a normal freight carrier. He tried to talk his way out of that recommendation as to the millions it cost them on their building. I think Asok cooled the issue a bit and we can use those ships. I wanted to keep you alerted to that situation. I'm sorry if I didn't get to you first and pass it by you since you are the ring leader."

"That's alright, Mr. President, I am aware of the situation. You should know however, that that conversion may cost us some time in delivery. It'll take us an additional time to get them on line."

"if I told you we don't have four months would you believe me? I know you are doing your best, but try to speed up your efforts before civilized society collapses on Zavre. These two extra ships will give you additional room for five-hundred passengers."

"Hell, Mr. President, Ani Shah's committee, who is deciding those passengers, will not be happy with that addition." Frisca smiled as if those additional passengers will be to his advantage. I hope not.

"On another matter, Mr. President, let me show you a tentative list that Ani Shah has put together of volunteers for her selection committee. I trust that you will okay the members."

Frisca glanced briefly at Shah's list, he was in the same boat as a million residents of the planet; he did not know if he or his family would be chosen. "Adam, now that you have additional ships you may be able to add some other families on this ride. You should alert Shah to my thought. I have not double- guessed your decisions and will not do it now. Ani's list is as good as it's goin' to get. I'm sure that her selections were done with knowledge of the requirements needed to survive intergalactic travel. Go with it, just throw Jacobs in the group; he's been calling me every two hours."

After brief handshakes, Adam left the President, Zak and Tomas. He immediately called Eve and Jonah. Leaving the same message with their secretaries, *"Speed up the work, we're running out of time."*

CHAPTER XIX

Adam returned Jonah's call which was picked up almost immediately. "Okay, Jonah, what's on your mind? I was tied up with the President and some contractors. You better have some interesting things to say."

Adam sensed Jonah's smile on the phone, "Well, everything is relative. My news is important but not nearly to the degree of yours. I hope my interruption did not eliminate my being a candidate?

"Believe it or not, I have some good news. First, the metallurgical engineers at Davis have discovered that a carbon fiber aluminum steel laminate can be used for the inside construction which is giving them both the lightness and the strength they require. This system has lowered the total weight of the space ship and will allow us to board the two hundred people. They could bring their toothbrushes and water bottles. They're also installing heavy insulation so we don't freeze in outer space or burn up when we re-enter the atmosphere. It gets pretty cold up there. We're currently installing the cooling units that Davis engineers suggested for our re-entry. One of their engineers has discovered, and it seems to work in the wind tunnel, is to attach solar sails to increase our speed."

"Okay, that's a plus," answered Adam, "What's the other good news?"

"Since the space ship has less weight than we had initially thought, my batteries will be more efficiently used to get us off this planet. I spoke to Eve before and she tells me that we should plan to push off within two months. It seems that is when we are closest to the sun. If we miss that date we'd have to wait another year. Knowing the condition of the population I don't know what will happen 'til then."

Adam interrupted any further words by Jonah, "Yes, Eve did mention that to me, but she was busy confirming her own problems and did not have the time to give me any details on this new development. It sounds great, now all we have to do is put all the pieces together. I just left the President's office to tell him that information. Bottom line... time becomes even more important. We have to get all of our sub-contractors on the same page with that date in mind. Something we have to keep in mind is we have to make sure that the food supplements are ready for the trip. I'm sure you're aware of the recent good news. Frisca convinced Ezra to use his two partially completed ships."

"Well," answered Jonah, that's good news and bad news. We were just catching up on our battery production and now this will set us back almost three weeks. We will have to change the whole interior of the two ships. They were designed as commercial cargo carriers, now they have to be converted to passenger carriers with seats. They will need at least two bathrooms set-ups and hand rails for safety when we lose gravity. You can see we'll have a lot of work to do."

"And the good news," Adam asked?

Jonah reviewed his notebook," we will use their work force. We can use Davis' two hundred technicians. That will be a great help."

"Could that change your delivery date?"

"I'm afraid not. I still have a couple of months to get re-organized."

"Well, Jonah, you better get your team coordinated. Eve just told Frisca that we have to be ready for push off in two months."

"Thanks, Adam for the tight schedule. Tell Eve I'll give her a wrench to push us along. I'll see you guys Sunday night to bring you up to date. Order some decent wine. You have anything else to add to this conversation?"

"Something we have to factor in is that once we choose her two hundred, they will have to go to school to learn how to live in a zero atmosphere. Davis says that would take five days. Another factor to keep in mind we have to make sure that the food supplements are ready for this trip. I'll call our food suppliers and tell them the good news. I'm sure they'll be over-joyed. I realize that this is playing it a little tight, but we have little choice."

≠

As Adam hung up from Jonah the phone rang again. It was Jackson Loren. *Thank God,* thought Adam, *if the food problem is not solved all the rest of the program will fall apart.*

"Hi there, Dr. Loren, I'm depending upon you for good news. How's Dr. Able holding up with all this stress?"

"Adam, I have some good news, the other bad. Abba could not stand the pressure put upon him and the company and not being assured he or his family would be chosen for this adventure of yours did himself in. He committed suicide two nights ago. After his family had dinner, he gave them a drink containing a lethal dose of some poison. His driver found them all this morning. I was so shaken up by his sudden decision that I couldn't talk to anyone...especially you. My God, I worked with this guy for forty years!"

"My God, I am sorry," answered Adam, "I would have thought he could have stayed the course. This is not the first time I've heard of one of our senior people taking a lethal drink or other means to take their lives. It hurts my heart but we have to carry on. But, since you called me, you must have some news to tell me. I hope it's good."

After a long pause, Loren answered, "I think we resolved the food problem. All the doctors examining the components finally agreed that the revised package would contain all the needed components to sustain energy. Your people are not going to get fat sipping on a half liter of enhanced food supplements…but that's the best we can do. You had an example of the size of the tablet we initially proposed it's not workable on our tablet presses. As we talk the machines are turning out liquids as fast as they can. It may take another month, working twenty-four hours a day, to produce a million, but that's the best we can do."

It was difficult for Adam to tell Dr. Loren the current development, but it had to be done. "I am really sorry to hear about your partner, Dr. Able. We hear of these tragedies every day. Dr. Loren, I have some good and bad news for you. The destination for our space ship has been re-discovered and we have to get off this planet in two months. It seems we have a time frame where the planet we are shooting for will be in its closest orbit to us. You've done a great job so far and I know I must be asking you too much but we require the food supply to be delivered to our space vehicle within two weeks. Is their any chance of your production doing this?"

"Adam, that is almost an impossible job. Not only are our filling machines working at full capacity but we will need the raw materials to go into the system. That may be the problem. I'll call our suppliers and try to get them to up their production, but, I know it will be a problem. We may not be able to reach our goal, but we'll get close. We will do our best. Good luck to your team...they will need it."

#

That night, Adam called Ani Shah, "Ani, it's a go, the President has okayed your list of committee members. You now will have two-hundred and fifty citizens to decide on. Just include Jacobs. When can you start your selection?

"Adam, the selection was not as easy as I thought it. I'm still working on the final list. Almost two dozen people who I contacted turned me down giving various reasons. As soon as they are available, it should take a couple of days. Wish me luck!"

"You got it."

Ani walked to her parking place, ready to drive home. Her head was in a different world. She got into her small two seater Scat and started to drive the three miles to her home when she noticed a black car following her. *Who could that be at this time of the night and he is driving almost on my tail!*

All of a sudden, the strange car pulled along side of hers and with the passenger's window open screamed, "You better put me on that damn committee of yours or your going to be in trouble." With that the man burnished a hand revolver. Ani felt her heart do a triple beat as she immediately put her foot on the brakes and allowed the stranger's car to shoot ahead of her. She was home in another five minutes shaking with fear.

She awoke, at three from a restless sleep, as if she had been hit on the head with a brick. The only person who would know about the committee and its members would be Jacobs. Would he threaten me? Ani laid back on her pillows, *that bastard. Is this what she should expect to get?*

#

Finally, after almost a week of frustration and rejection at one-thirty in the morning, with a list of ten in her case she called Adam. After the third ring, Adam picked up the phone. Ani interrupted any words that were forthcoming, "Adam, I know it is late, but I have my members who will choose your passengers. As soon as you give me the go-ahead and let me know what the total passenger number will be, I can go ahead. Sleep tight." She hung up. *Why should I be the only one up at this ungodly time.*

On Friday, promptly at nine, Ani Shah walked into Adam's office. "Well Adam, I have to tell you I worked almost a week preparing that committee list, I hope it's in time before our people go crazy. You know, Doctor, that preparing this list almost got me killed."

"Really, what happened?"

"I did not want to tell you but the other night I was threatened by a gunman to include him on the committee.

I have the gut feeling that it was either Jacobs or one of his friends. Can you imagine? It may be a coincidence but Jacobs called me this morning telling me his problems and opinions for this ethical committee. He stated in positive terms that he should be a contributing member if not the chairperson. I was all ready to quit this high paying job and then I thought, who would replace me? Screw him---no-one intimidates a Shah."

"Well I'm glad you did. Let's look at your final list; the one I showed Frisca was okay." Ani removed from her purse the sheet of paper containing the names. You will notice that I included a few women in the list, it should give some balance." Both Ani and Adam glanced at the final list and nodded.

"Thanks a million for sticking with the program, Ani, when will you be able to start your meetings?"

"Give me a couple of weeks."

"Ani, I'm afraid you don't have that much time, we gotta be outa here in five weeks.."

CHAPTER XX

Adam, as instructed, was at the President's private eating quarters at seven eating a hot bun and sipping some juice while giving his update on the current progress of the space ship. The weather was noticeably cooler. It was not uncommon to see the population now dressed in coats, jackets, hats and gloves although according to the calendar it was late spring. President Frisca, who would normally appear in a freshly pressed suit and tie to match, would now join him in a sport shirt, heavy sweater, unshaven. The pressure of his responsibility was definitely affecting him.

"No Sir, I haven't read anything in the papers nor have I seen anything on TV. I just know what's happening in the city. It's not very pleasant."

"We've been trying to keep this type of news out of the media, but once in awhile some wise reporter leaks the story. This was a delicate matter that was discussed at a Cabinet meeting. The census was to keep the news off the airways and papers. All it would achieve would be additional mayhem. Half of our world is under martial law already. We live in difficult times, Adam; you have to get this space ship ready to go before there is complete insanity. I do not think you realize the extent of the cooling situation."

"I realize what you are saying and are preparing for that, Mr. President; we have increased security where we are assembling the space ships. Ezra Davis, CEO of Davis Engineering, has already told me of some nasty incidents. We are expecting the first delivery of food within the next few days. I hope their trucks can get into the assembly plant. The new batteries are being installed as we speak. We may need some militia to patrol the site. You're right, Sir, things are liable to get violent."

The President took a deep breath as if he were counting his words, "Adam, do you think that my family would have a chance to be selected to leave Zavre? I'm not talking about myself and my wife, but I have two sons and their families. I wouldn't like to have my family tree left on this dead planet. Does this committee of Shah's have any criteria of who to select for this trip? You have any thoughts on this?"

"Mr. President, I don't know if I and Eve will be selected. I do know that Shah has basic requirements for the passengers. Age, experiences, ability to live in a strange environment are just a few that I am aware of. I'm afraid we'll all have to wait. I can tell you this; I'd hate to be on that committee to make those decisions."

"You know it is quite amazing, Adam, a member of our Congress called the other day and asked where had all the water has gone. He owned a yacht, and previously his boat would pull right up to his dock. The ocean now is a hundred feet from his docks. When he asked, 'Where is the water,' I had trouble convincing him that the water has gone into ice sheets and glaciers. I think he thought I was crazy. A final blow to me happened yesterday when one of our top marine biologist give me a summary of the reduction in coral, a major factor in fish growth. Go know."

Adam had to smile, "I guess it takes the realities of life to convince some people we were not fooling with our findings. Is there anything else, Mr. President?"

The President's response was final; he just waved Adam goodbye as he left the room.

CHAPTER XXI

Unfortunately, Adam realized there remained a number of almost equally important projects that had to be resolved or brought up to date and Jonah and his vital battery projects was one of the most important one.

"Hi, Jonah, it's Adam, are you still there? It's Friday night, go home and have a beer. Are you prepared for our big meeting Sunday night?"

"Of course I'm still here, where would you expect me to be? With all the responsibilities that you lay on me how can I relax? What ya call for? We just spoke last week and I gave you an up-to-date summary on what's goin' on in my group."

"Can I get to see you Sunday? I think that you and I and Eve should compare notes. We are getting down to the bitter end with this program of ours and I think all of us together will clear any confusions. Besides, I have confidence that you have good news for me."

"What makes you think Adam that I have good news for you? I've been sending you reports almost weekly about any good news that I may have."

"Com'n Jonah, now that you have an open-ended expense account and have all the top brains on the planet working for you, you should be coming back to me with fantastic results. Your reports have as much new information as do kindergarten kids. What kind of a report is that? By the way, when was the last time you had a full night's sleep or a decent meal?"

"Since I last saw you, almost a hundred years ago or at least since you told me your ideas. I'd love to see you Sunday, but we'll be finishing a detailed study on a three-way alloy composite system that's looking promising. I'd like to be there for the final testing. Sorry."

"I had a brief meeting with Ruben James a couple of weeks ago and he told me that they were starting to install your new batteries. That sounded like good news."

"I'm afraid, Adam, that James was a little optimistic. We are doing some measurements, but installations...not yet. Good try, however. Give me another month."

"I'm afraid that a couple of weeks won't make it. We need additional speed, but how about a late dinner? Say seven-thirty? We can meet at that diner down the street from your lab. Is it a go? That'll save you some travel time. I have a number of important things to discuss with you."

"You're cutting into my work day, but yes, I think I can spare my boss an hour or so." The line went dead.

#

The following day, at four o'clock, Adam realized that he hadn't spoken to Eve that day. As usual she was back in her office trying to coordinate the results of ten other labs. She was gone before he had finished his shower. He forgot to tell her about their dinner meeting with Jonah that evening.

"Jebba, get Eve on the phone, please."

Almost instantly from the outer office, Jebba responded, "Eve is on the phone, Dr.Andros."

"Okay Adam, what's up? I'm up to my neck in problems, what's so important to catch me in the middle of a three way conversation with two other labs. They insist that my calculations and interpretations are incorrect. These are people who have been in this business for years. How can I argue with them?"

"Are you available for Sunday night with Jonah, I'd like to hear how he's doing with his project. Are you aware that we have two more ships hijacked from Davis Engineering.? It seems our Pres put a job on them and they agreed. Like to hear the whole gossip"?

"You betcha."

"See you Sunday."

"I have a conference on Sunday with two other astrophysicists from other observatories who want to compare notes. This is a meeting I can't miss."

"I'm afraid you're going to have to change your dinner plans. I planned to meet Jonah for dinner at seven-thirty. We will be meeting in that little restaurant around the corner from his lab. If it has power use the car, I'll use the walk/jog method. Please try to make it. It's tough being with him alone. He depresses me."

"Okay, I'll have to change my dinner meeting with those two heaven seekers for the following evening. They won't be happy, but Jonah comes first. I'll be there but a little late. Thanks for letting me use the car; it will save me some time. I have to go home to change my clothes and wash up. I've had a busy, busy day. Fortunately, I have some good news."

"Really, should you tell me now about your good news?"

"I'm confirming our findings right now. See ya later." The phone went dead.

Holy smokes, Adam thought *that is the second time that I've been hung up on. Things must be looking up.*

#

"The Continental," was an up-scale fast-food restaurant in the best traditions of the Capitol City. Almost all locals guaranteed that the food served was the best of its type in the city. Owned by the Gramaldi family for three generations, they continued to serve the freshest salads and the best synthetic steaks, meat loaf and patties on Zavre. Forty years before, their grandmother had discovered that a blend of chopped string beans, finely ground onions, soy beans, peas and mushrooms would both taste and appear as meat and, when properly spiced, they were correct. The restaurant had 12 tables that were served by solicitous young waitresses employed from the University. For a restaurant of its size and type, it had an unusually fine selection of wines. Its nice intimate appearance appealed to a select clientele.

With the bus system not running on it's regular,schedule due to the inability to re-charge it's batteries, Adam took the mile walk to the Continental to meet his diner companions. He arrived fifteen minutes earlier but three staff members who quizzed him about rumors about a space ship being built stopped him in the entrance. "Was it true, what we are hearing? Are we really going to be leaving Zavre?"

All he could say was that they were examining all possibilities and some progress was being made. Their demeanor to that response indicated their disbelief. One of the researchers, a young man in his late twenties, continued, "My God, Doc, I'm supposed to get married in a couple of months. We don't know what to do. Any suggestions?"

"Get married Andre, please send us an invitation." That brief lie seemed to pacify Andre.

Although it was relatively early in the evening, the sun's rays were slightly masked and it was noticeably cooler for this time of the year. He noticed a few couples on the street walking arm in arm, dressed with light sweaters or jackets. Adam thought to himself, *in two years they'll be walking these streets with overcoats.* Adam, walking at a fast clip, noted as the sun dipped towards the horizon, a faint unaccustomed chill reaching him. He should have worn a heavier jacket. What the scientists had been discussing climate change the past three plus years was, in fact, obvious— it was getting chilly.

The restaurant was on the other side of the city closer to Jonah's laboratories and his living quarters. Surprisingly, the restaurant was almost empty. Even then, Adam was able to talk the owner into a table in the far rear. He knew their conversations were not for the mass public's ears. Knowing that he may need some ammunition to temper Jonah's negativity, Adam ordered a reasonably priced bottle of red wine. He had a few sips as he awaited their arrival.

Twenty minutes after seven, Jonah showed wearing a ratty old shirt and jacket with chemical burns, food and coffee stains adorning the front. He appeared as if he hadn't shaved in a week. His usual well-groomed, shorn hair hadn't been touched in months and fell over the collar of his shirt and rested on his shoulders. His jeans had the rest of the stains that had missed his shirt. Adam shook his head in amazement; his most dependable scientist looked like a worn out street bum.

Adam was afraid to shake his hand fearing that Jonah's germs would leap from the filthy body to his. He just said, "My God, Jonah, I haven't seen you in a number of months and you look like crap. What the hell is wrong with you? We have to do something about your appearance." With no immediate response from Jonah, who just sat down at the table and stared into the void, Adam quickly added, "Have a drink. Maybe that will put some light in your eyes. It's your favorite booze."

Jonah Blanca took a deep breath and exhaled as if it were his last. "Adam, you are one big pain. First, you give me an impossible task to resolve, second, you put me on a time frame, and third", looking at the label on the wine bottle, "this wine is the worst. Who said it's my favorite? But, I'll take it." And with that remark, he filled a wine goblet, and before Adam could add another word, he gulped the wine in one long swallow. Jonah put the wine goblet down with a bang that shook the other glasses on the table, gave a slight smile, and said, "How ya been, Boss? It's good to see ya! Ya look like you've seen better days." It was his first words of greeting. Adam had to grin. He realized that Jonah remarks were out of frustration and over-work. But knowing his intellect and determination, he would come around.

"I gather you had a good day," Adam said, following with a smile.

"Now that you mention it, I've had a couple of pretty productive weeks, and I have some promising news that may cost you a dinner. Where's Eve?"

"She will be here shortly; she was changing her clothes in your honor which I see was unnecessary. When was the last time you had a shower, Jonah, you're smellin' up the place."

Jonah laughed, "I thought this was to be a business meeting, not a social event, but, to answer your question, about a week ago." Adam just scrunched up his nose as Eve entered the restaurant and seeing the two men, walked to the table. She planted a slight kiss on Jonah's forehead. "My God, Jonah, you smell terrible and you look even worse. When was the last time you washed your hair?"

"Don't get too romantic with him, Eve, he might take it seriously," Adam said with a smile. Except for a small clock chiming on the wall, the three, once again, remained quiet. Then Eve continued, "You know, we've spoken about batteries and engineering problems but we haven't even considered food! How do you plan to feed these people?"

"Under control, I've been in contact with Abba Able yesterday. He was their chief engineer responsible for food production. They told me this morning that he and his family done themselves in. A great guy, we will miss him. Their company will be making enhanced liquid foods for us that will nourish the passengers. They moaned and groaned over the time limits I put on them but I believe they will come around. Jackson Loren, their head marketing man will now be the lead. Unfortunately, he doesn't know anything about our requirements. Their chief research engineers have left the company and now they have to work with a reduced staff. Their job is not an easy one. We had to compromise and use a liquid food system. This may take up more room than we would like, but it would be more efficient. You think you have a problem? Not very palatable but it's the only other method we could consider. This part of the program normally would take a couple of years Corporation Drug will have to complete this in three or four months. Well, Eve, are you done quizzing me, I'd like to get to the reason for this meeting."

Jonah poured Eve a glass of wine and another large glass of wine for himself, smiled, "I just had that discussion with your boy friend. Can we order and then talk business? I have to get back to my lab to confirm some interesting results."

"Interesting results? Interesting results? I love to hear favorable results," answered Adam, "I don't get them too often these days."

Eve just answered, "I hope your results are as good as mine, I think we have a target to shoot for." Both men looked at her with anticipation. As the waiter approached to take their orders, all three refilled their glasses and sat back in their chairs, trying to relax; it had been a long day.

#

The two men ordered faux meat dinners, while Eve, sticking to her diet, ordered a salad with light dressing. Their conversation was stilted. When they did converse, it was not about the subject of the meeting but inter-lab gossip, conditions in the government and the good service they were receiving. Both Eve and Jonah added the almost daily loss of their technicians. Many had the attitude,'What's the use,' while others wanted to spend their last days or years with their families. Jonah added the fact that a dozen of his best people had committed suicide rather than face the future. This news brought their conversation to a complete halt for some minutes. They ate quickly and desperately as if they had other things on their minds. Adam finally said something pertinent to the dinner, "You guys want another bottle of wine? I can charge it as a business expense. You two do remember I have an unlimited expense account."

Jonah answered, with his usual bravado, "That would be a great idea, but I have to get back to the lab to see some final results; how about holding that bottle for our next get together."

Eve looked about the almost empty room and remarked, so quietly to the two men that they had to lean forward to catch her words, "In walking here I couldn't help but notice how empty the streets were. Usually at this time of night they would be jammed with couples out on dates and just strolling about. The numbers of peoples are depleted. I'd rather not say where all the people are going. I hope you fellows notice how these people are dressed. In normal times these streets would be crowded with people in summer clothing. All they would be wearing, at this time of the evening, would be a light blouse or shirt. Almost everyone has a jacket or sweater. The temperature, people, is rearing its ugly head."

Adam answered, almost apologetically, "You're right. I received a report this afternoon saying that the average temperature has dropped a five full degrees from last year. Almost ten degrees from five years. Ice mass is building at the poles not seen in our lifetime. People are getting worried and nervous. The farm unions are besieging the President with complaints and requests for answers. I hope we don't run out of time." They sat in silence digesting the implication of this news.

Jonah joined the conversation with a story that took his friends heart. "I was coming out of my office when this well dressed man approached and asked if I worked there. When I said, "Yes," he offered me a large sum of money. During the conversation he claimed it was five hundred thousand quadros. He thought I had a position in the administration to be able to get his family on this ship we were building. He could not believe I had no authority to do this and I did not know if I would be a passenger. His response was he would increase his offer to one million quadros, if I could introduce him to anyone who would help him. When I once again, told him I had no authority and turned him down, he burst into tears and ran down the street. My heart went out to him. I guess we can expect such further actions from our citizens." It was deadly quiet in the room. Tears ran down Eve's cheeks.

After a few minutes of utter stillness, a waitress broke the stillness and served their drinks and desserts and left the immediate scene, Adam started the conversation, "Jonah, I do not not know why you haven't told the team the news of us now having three ships to get off the planet. If Eve is not aware, and I have not seen her for two days, a couple of days ago Frisca laid the law on Davis demanding that two of his ships be converted to passenger space ships. After some hair pulling, Ezra James okayed the demand. We now have three ships to build or re-build.

I talked to Jonah about the advantages and disadvantages and it seems to be a wash. The only advantages to us is that we now can carry seven-hundred fifty passengers and we have their technical help. Otherwise, Jonah has to produce more batteries and my Chair lady for the Ethical Committee will have additional headaches choosing passengers...

Eve stopped Adam at that point, "What is the advantage? If we take two hundred survivors or seven hundred? More than a million will be left here?"

"I don't know, Eve, maybe Frisca believes his family will have a better chance of being chosen. If I know Ani Shah, she'll choose by talents and ability than by numbers and political pressures. The bottom line to all this is we probably have an extra two weeks before push off time. I hope, Eve that this will not cause us to miss our window for launch."

"Launch time is still set, Adam, all you need now is three pilos, not one. Good luck, Jonah."

Jonah's shoulders dropped two inches; the sides of his mouth dropped another half inch, "Adam you're going to kill me. My energy plans would be to carry one hundred at the most. To get power to lift two-fifty would throw all my developmental work out the window. Adam, it's almost impossible. The President's getting involved with the transportation and how it's going to affect power requirements was out of order. His number is equally out of the question. Davis's figure is bad, but at least workable. He breathed deeply, after finishing the last sips of wine in his glass. "And I was going to tell you the good news that our most recent investigations have proven successful and we can now improve our energy source and miniaturization by one hundred fold. We have field tested our most current battery system and, lo and behold, it works. These new plastic/metal combinations have increased energy output almost one thousand percent and reduced its size considerably. Our sub-contractors are currently making these units and almost a half dozen have already been installed. This would be great for one hundred people, possibly two hundred but two-fifty is ridiculous. Can we scale back our optimism? I think I will order that extra bottle of wine now." He signaled to the waitress.

The bottle arrived; this time it was approved by Jonah, and after the glasses were refilled to a quiet, pensive table, Adam responded, although he was not sure where this discussion was going, "Let me get down to the gory story. The administration put a lot of heat on Davis Engineering and Ezra finally gave in. He knows he will not be among those chosen to take the trip. So basically he gave up a couple of million invested in his two ships, have them converted to passengers ships and be a hero to Frisca. Maybe he'll get a medal."

"Adam, I'll been frank with you, whatever you said I'm sure is correct, but it is all political. I still need to get this ship off the ground. Two hundred is a max number; I can probably live with it, but barely. Those hundred will have to be aware that all they will be allowed to take on board is a minimum of personal effects. In fact we would probably have to weigh everyone. Not a great thought. It would pay to be skinny. I'm joking, Eve, but it would be tight.. Without getting involved in the math involved, for every pound that you put on the ship would require a specific energy to throw us out of the gravity forces holding us down here. It's basic math. Our engineers have developed charts in our lab showing weight versus energy requirements to get us off this planet and the necessary survival equipment. Have James get me the weight of the space ship, maybe we can compromise somewhere. Even if we can save 50,000 pounds it would help. In a guess, we will need two million pounds of thrust on lift off." Jonah sat back in his chair, exhausted. He hadn't spoken so forcefully since his college days.

Adam looked at Eve, "Please tell me something good, Honey."

Eve pushed the remainder of her diet dessert from one side of the plate to the other. Finally she looked up, her blue-grey eyes blazing. "After hearing all of this from Jonah, I feel depressed. But to bring you up-to-date, over the past months we have been zeroing in on a location that I initially thought had some possibility. With the increased misting situation it became more difficult to get an exact point but for the past few weeks one of our observatories confirmed our highest hopes. They received a strong blip on our screens indicating there may be a planet out there that could be habitable. This was confirmed by three other labs stationed throughout our planet, so it is a positive sign. Our radio-magnetic devices indicate that in our galaxy a planet exists that may contain the air and water we require to exist. It is in a solar system in a quadrant we have been closely screening for the past years prior to this misting situation."

Jonah interrupted, "Is this a new location?"

"Yes and no. We had evidence that something was there, but for the past months we were trying to narrow down the exact area. We finally were able to get a more exact reading and fine tune the quadrant and receive a stronger confirmation. Last month, it appeared again. It appears that it is traveling in it's own orbit around our own sun. We've been monitoring it for a month to make sure it was not an error. There are so many stars in the Milky Way it is very easy to confuse those in our orbit or those flying by. This is for real guys. This was the same general area that we had discussed a million days ago. I believe we have a direction and a site to shoot for. It seems to be, at this time, a light year away. The only problem is that it is in its own orbit and that orbit ranges in depth from one light year to two. I'm hoping, of course, that when we start getting closer to blast-off time, the object will be closer to one than to two. I have to remind you that a light year is six trillion miles. That is not just a short walk in the park. We still would have a long way to go."

They were quiet for a couple of seconds and then Jonah removed a small calculator from his shirt pocket. For thirty seconds he pressed a series of numbers on the unit and then said, "With the best speed we can put forth, it would take eighty years to get there if the planet is one light year away. If it's four; forget about it."

"Where did you get those numbers, Jonah?" questioned Eve.

"I've been doing some reading about space travel and the speed of space ships in science fiction magazines and using the speeds that they discuss, that's the figure. They mention that the faster you go the slower time becomes. It is a subject I know nothing about. I hope that our pilot is more knowledgeable in this area."

"My consultants tell me," answered Eve, "that there is some type of a relationship between the mass and the speed of light. The bottom line is, my friend, Jonah, we should be more positive. We don't know how fast we will be able to travel, especially with your added energy. Some of my assistants question, 'How do you measure speed in outer space?' Others believe that this planet may be coming towards us so that it may not be that far away as we imagine. We will not be able to determine that until we leave Zavre. It is something, however, that we are praying for. But at least, I've done my job, I found a place to go, let's talk optimistically about getting there."

"Okay, let me get on the happiness wagon of yours. How big does this new universe of yours seem to be?"

"It's hard to tell. This planet of mine spins around our sun as we do but in a completely different orbit in an elliptical fashion. This is why sometimes it is closer to us and sometimes further. We were able to determine that it does have an atmosphere containing water and oxygen, a good sign. It is, however, slightly larger than our planet, which, in fact, may be to our advantage; but who knows. Be that as it may, that's the one we should be shooting for, as if we have a choice."

"Does it seem to be populated?" Adam asked.

"Not that we can tell. If it is, they must be not nearly as advanced in technology as we are. We've received no response when we bombarded them with radio waves and signals. They can just be an immature civilization."

"Or none at all!"

"Could be."

The table, once again, was still, everyone thinking their own thoughts. It was Jonah who broke the ice with a smile as big as his heart, "Maybe this is the wine talking, but damn it Adam, we may be able to pull this off after all. We may not be able to get to Eve's crazy planet of hers, but we'll be sure kept busy." He raised his wine glass in a toast to Adam. "Ya know, when you thought of this wacko project, I really thought that you were just doing this to keep our minds busy while we waited to freeze to death. Your craziness may work yet."

Adam swirled the wine around in his glass watching the amber wine form rings, "Jonah, thanks for the accolades, but we still have a million things to resolve. One, Eve, do not mention an exact destination for our ships, let's keep that under wraps for a while. Second, blasting off Zavre, escaping gravity and becoming weightless and then finding this planet that Eve hopefully has discovered may be the easy task; getting the people on this planet to go along with our plans may be more difficult. I am sure that the million or so people who will be left on Zavre will not be too happy."

Eve answered, with a choked voice, "We could be in for some interesting and tragic times."

It was quiet at the table as the three friends sipped their wine and considered their own possible responses to the messages that Adam had presented.

Then suddenly Jonah broke the awkward silence, "Okay, guys, let me show you something."

He bent over and removed from his carrying case a picture; perhaps a six by eight inch in color. He threw it on the table with Eve picking it up immediately saying, “What is this? It looks like three quarters of a cut off tennis ball.”

Before Adam could add his words, Jonah interrupted Eve, “C’mon, Eve, look carefully because this is a picture of one of the ships that Ezra Davis is completing that will take us away from Zavre.”

Adam finally got in his words, “Holy smoke, Jonah, Eve is right what you are showing me is not a plane or a ship but half a ball. It’s nothing I’ve seen before.”

“Well,” answered Jonah, “you are not an aeronautical engineer or designer. Our authority in the area, Ruben James says this design will give us the strength and mobility we will need and has the space for two hundred you are considering.”

Eve shook her head in disgust, “it still doesn’t look as if it can fly.”

Jonah took a deep breath and his words exploded with some disgust,” If we would have had more time we would have done some additional flight testing, but your need for speed prevailed and kept us from doing them. We only could do a couple of flight simulations.”

Eve continued her thoughts,” So what are the chances that this monster of a plane will not fly.”

"Eve, I don't want to even think about that. I only showed you this picture to show you that these ships should be ready in a couple of weeks...get moving."

"What is that attached to the outside of the ship, Jonah?"

"That is where my ring of thirty six batteries will be placed. These will be my present to you for considering this crazy project. Next to them are the heat shields and next to them are cooling elements. Ruben James has assured me that everything on this vehicle has been designed for use and utility. No one else has seen this picture. Right now they are completing the inside. Gentlemen, lades, we have come a long way in five years."

Adam, once again, looked at Jonah's photo, "It still looks ugly."

Jonah laughed, "beauty will not get us where we want to go. We chose Davis because they knew what they were doing."

"My God, Jonah, do you have any idea what this monster has cost us?"

"Eve took the last bit of her salad and said, with a smile," you better move on this, Jonah, we're running out of time and the ship should be ready shortly."

"You must be kidding me," Jonah answered. "No one on Zavre has the experience to fly such a monstrous plane. But

I'll speak to Ruben James about this and he should know all the pilots on Zavre. He should know the best man available and who has piloted commercial transports. I will contact him within the week. He better not turn me down."

"Why," answered Eve "will they have another job?"

The team surpressed a smile.

"Just to add to your timetable, Jonah, I'm sure that your pilots will have to study up on the piloting of such a huge ship. This could take a couple of weeks for them to learn the ropes."

"Okay, Boss I catch you're message, as of tomorrow, I'll do my search and find routine and get us a pilot."

"Adam," Jonah responded, "finish your drink and let's finish this crazy business. I gotta look for some pilots!"

CHAPTER XXII

For the next two days, Jonah spent all his time contacting every senior pilot on the planet. Quite surprisingly there were only a half dozen who had the experience that was required. Unfortunately, four were drunks and two others had families they did not want to leave. The one qualified with all the experiences needed was working as an independent researcher and had retired from flying two years before. It was this ex-pilot that Jonah felt had the most to offer He called Adam, "Adam, I think I got our pilot. Do you want to talk to him. He's a strange one, but capable. He was recommended by Davis."

"Does he have any friends"?

"I guess I'll find out."

Adam just shrugged his shoulders, "If you feel he has the experience— go with him. I have too many issues on my plate to get involved in that area, and from what you say, we don't have too many choices. Just remember that your pilots will have to study up on the piloting of such a huge ship. This could take a couple of weeks for him to learn the ropes."

Two days later, Jonah borrowing Adam's small car, drove to a site miles from the city. There he had been told the major airplane manufacturers and ships were repaired and built. The facilities were tremendous; the plant area could have been a mile long.

Jonah knocked on the wood door of the huge hanger with no response. He knocked again with similar results-no results-none Finally, taking his aggressiveness to use, he opened the door and stepped into a huge airplane hanger of tremendous size; perhaps one hundred by two hundred yards.

Inside, supported by huge steel beams was two partially completed airplanes. Almost every foot of space was covered with tools, machine parts and other metal parts. Jonah had no idea what these devices were used for. He just stared at the half completed ships that almost dwarfed the building. Jonah glanced at the planes and thought, workers running about, some on the ships, some in the ships. The dim was deafening. Everyone was calling for equipment and help. Instead of expressing his opinion out loud, he shouted," Anyone home."

A voice from the deep rear of the hanger answered, "Cool it, mister. I heard you knock the first time. Give me a sec."

In two minutes, Jonah was joined by a short, bald-headed man who appeared to be in his mid-fifties. His work overalls were covered with grease and oil residue. "Okay, who the hell are you and what are you doing in a secure area."

Jonah stuck out his hand, "I'm Jonah Blanca and as of now I work for the government. I was told I could find a Yari Roebling at this location. Is that you?"

"Well, you're right in a couple of matters. I am Roebling and if you are the person I was expecting you are Jonah Blanca. If we are on the same page, you should have been here about a year ago. But let by-gones be by-gones, what can I do for you and this crazy company. Right now I'm being paid almost five times my regular pay to get these boats in the air. I doubt as if this ship will ever get off the ground. You're costing me money; talk fast."

"I guess I am the one to tell you that I am authorized by the President to talk to you. You should listen as it involves you and according to Davis Engineering you are the person we need."

Yari leaned against a uncompleted section of the airplane and with a question in his voice replied, "Rueben James!, those cheap sob's, they still owe me money for my last job. What lies did they tell ya about me? What do you have for me?"

"Yari, Rueben claims you are the best test pilot on the planet, but as of now you are authorized by the President to pilot one of our proposed space ships. This ship is currently under construction by Davis."

Although it was bedlam in the plant, it was quiet between the two men. Yari finally broke the silence, "You're kiddin' me, I've been retired for two years, find another pilot."

"I'm afraid not, Yari, this is no joking matter and tomorrow morning you and I will visit Davis who will bring you up to date on what's goin' on."

"My God, Jonah, Davis is expecting me to drop my engineering job here and pilot this ship. You may not know it, but two years ago I put this ship together. You are expecting me to drop all for some wild thoughts of piloting a space craft which we know nothing about? You're kiddin.'"

"Yari, I will let Ezra Davis explain our predicament and our need for you."

"Jonah, two points here. One, I gather that this crises that requires me has something to do with the fogging situation we are having. Secondly, your project is an impossible one. It will take me almost a year to study and learn all about this ship you are currently trying to build. It normally would take two to three years. I have to learn every nut, bolt and movement of the ship...it can't be done!"

"Yari, I currently have hundreds of various engineers working on these ships with the attitude.'It can't be done.' Yari, it can be done and you will help us do it. I will meet you at Davis Engineering tomorrow at ten. I will need two additional pilots. Bring them along." He turned and left the hanger before Yari could ask another question. Yari just stood there an amazed look on his face.

That evening, Yari called three of his top engineers. They all were amazed their Boss was ignorant of the extent of the fog crises and had not been contacted before.

“Yari,” one of them explained.” what they are asking you to do is crazy. It will take you a year to learn the inner workings of this new ship.”

“Your right, Yonni, and I’m sure my visit with our mutual friend tomorrow, Davis will outline what is expected of us. Oh, I didn’t tell you guys, I expect you two to be with me.” He laughed.

Yari’s two assistants just moaned.

CHAPTER XXIII

Two days after her meeting with Adam, Ani, called her eleven commission members. She scheduled a preliminary meeting the next day to get the ball rolling. She realized from Adam's tone that time was critical, and knew she probably had the most sensitive, delicate job put before her. Ani told each member to come to the meeting with a list containing one hundred names of individuals who could meet their standards. She indicated that those nominated should have work experience in select areas and expertise in the fields of their endeavors. It was nice to be a dancer, a musician, an artist, a philosopher, a social worker but would they make it in the world that they may have to civilize. She did not go into any further details. She hoped they understood where she was coming from.

#

At one o'clock, just before her scheduled meeting, the phone ring...it was Adam. "Ani, I should have given you the current passenger status. We are now the owners of three ship that can hold seven-hundred fifty passengers. Anyway your group want to handle it is okay with me. You could use a lottery system we discussed if you believe that will work or have some advantage. Anyway, go get em; just keep me informed.

"This is not going to make everyone happy, but the President and his advisors believe this is the way to go. Do what you have to do at your meeting this afternoon."

"I'll let you know as soon as possible how this group handles that news." She hung up the phone. *My God, that is terrible, her selection of passengers will have to be completely revised. This is not goin' to be good.*

At one-thirty that afternoon, eleven men and women showed up at her office and were escorted by Ani's secretary into her large meeting room. Twelve chairs surrounded a large, highly polished table. Before each chair was a notebook and a handful of pens and pencils. On the far side of the room was a huge end table with urns filled with beverages. Large serving dishes were displayed containing finger cakes and sandwiches. Ani had prepared for a long, involved and probably confrontational meeting.

Four women from various colleges and universities were part of the group. Three were young to middle aged ladies with a wide experience in human behavior, social interaction with psychological backgrounds. One was a retired senior court judge. Three senior men were CEOs of the largest firms on the planet. Their extensive experiences were administrative.

Two had served on President Frisca's cabinet. Noah Jacobs was considered within that group. James Robinson was the President of Johnson University, a man of worldwide renown and respect. Sam Samuels, a gentleman, still erect, still alert in his 80's, a renowned astrologer in his early years, was the past President of Zavre. Frisca had replaced him as President. The last two were men with experience in engineering and manufacturing who could understand the manufacturing problems involved. Their companies were supplying Davis with the necessary equipment to build this space ship.

As they were milling about the imposing dark paneled room, introducing themselves, Jacobs quietly inched his way around the huge black mahogany table and sat just to the left where Ani Shah would be seated. He, in affect, indicated by his seating position, that he was her right hand man. Ani noticed this sleight of hand but rather than make an issue of his arrogance, just said, "Gentlemen, ladies, all seats are honored, please take a seat so that we may start these proceedings."

Sitting in the front seat, Ani formally introduced the members of the committee and gave a ten second briefing on their experience and background and why they had been chosen. Although everyone in the room knew the qualifications of all the members, everyone nodded in agreement as to her choices. There were no comments as to who were or not chosen.

With some hesitancy, Ani began what she knew would be a long, strenuous and frustrating ordeal, the selection of who shall take the unknown arduous trip. "Gentlemen, ladies, we have a most difficult task; we must choose seven-hundred and fifty people to board a space ship to leave this planet. To give you some time-frame, we must submit a list of those individuals within a few days. Time is our enemy here; so do not expect to leave this office until some major progress is made along those lines. All of you are aware that this planet is getting progressively cooler. Our scientists predict within ten years Zavre will be completely covered in ice. This planet, for all intents and purposes, will not be livable. As I speak, three space ships are being assembled to allow seven-hundred fifty of our citizens to leave and our responsibility is to choose two-fifty. You may question why two-fifty and my response is two-fold. This group will choose two-fifty and an additional five-hundred will be chosen randomly. But more on that later. I won't discuss why two-fifty. That is a number I derived after reviewing all of your base recommendations. Once again, we will return to that concept. I'm sure that there are some in the group who will vehemently disagree with my approach. We are here to select those lucky two-fifty. Speaking off the record, I do not know if those two-fifty individuals will be the lucky ones. They will be traveling to a hostile environment with unknown and dangerous problems of which they will have no experiences. And this will be after they have traveled perhaps five or ten years in a space ship in which some of them may not be able to survive intergalactic travel. Whoever they may be, we all wish them well. That is all we can do. They will need it."

With that last remark from Ani, Noah Jacobs leaped off his seat, "I'm afraid, Madam Chair lady that you should give us some reasoning why are we to chose two-hundred fifty and not the seven-fifty that the ships can carry?"

"Okay, Senator Jacobs, let's start with answering your question. I have spoken informally with the Director of this project, Dr. Adam Andros. He suggested, as a starting place, that we select one hundred citizens that would be of major help in the development of a new civilization and the remainder to be chosen from the general population selected via a general lottery. We believe this would be a most democratic way to select this group. We realize that this is a difficult job but, as someone told me, someone has to do it. May we start off with that compromise?"

Before Ani could even finish her opening statement, Jacobs continued his diatribe, "you speak quite eloquently, Dr. Shah, however you are not allowing this group to discuss this compromise of yours and its meaning. You must admit to send five hundred third rate citizens to an unknown planet and expect them to civilize it is a stretch of the imagination. What I would strongly vote for is that we choose the five hundred that have all the qualities that you specifically mentioned and their families, then, and only then, would those members have a chance to survive in a new world. The remainder two-fifty would be on the lottery list."

Ignoring Jacobs's remarks, Ani continued her introduction. "Let us start from the beginning, if all of you will give me your recommendations, I will give them to my secretary to put in the computer and see which names come out consistently. Perhaps in that way we can expedite this process." There was some crinkling of papers as the members removed from their jackets or cases the lists that Ani had asked them to prepare. "But to respond to Senator Jacobs thoughts, does anyone have a comment on my compromise?"

Sam Samuels raised his hand seeking recognition. Ani immediately said, "Mr. President, we welcome and respect any comments you may offer."

The ex-President, now in his late eighties, a man of dignity, with years of experience and knowledge answered, "Dr. Shah, allow an old man to address this problem without bias. At my age, I would not expect to be considered one of the passengers on the ship.

"With that said, although I can agree with the Senator's statement, we have always lived in a democratic society of one form or the other and to eliminate the third-rate citizen, as the fine Senator suggests, would be against all the principles of Zavre. Personally, I would like to see five hundred of the savants be chosen, if we can find that many, and two-fifty average citizens." The members of the committee laughed at his attempt at a joke.

Once again, Jacobs jumped to his feet and slapped his hand on the table violently, which caused some of the goblets and glasses on the table to rattle, "While I have great respect for our ex-President, a snide remark about finding five-hundred capable members in our society is an insult to our people. I am disappointed in your comments, Sir. We have many more than that citizens who can fill those few seats with the intelligence and experience that will be needed. President Samuels, with due respect, you are off base."

Ani could immediately see it was Jacobs who convinced Frisca to pirate the other two ships. He was hoping that his family would have a better chance to be taken in a group of seven-fifty than two hundred. Adam did say that politics always becomes a factor.

Ani interrupted the flow of raised hands, "I would appreciate that before you address the Chair, get recognized by its Chairperson. Senator, please do not speak out of order... again."

Jacobs, not willing to become subservient to Shah, remaining his feet and in a bellicose tone answered, "As Senator, I do not expect to be just an observer to these discussions. I expect to take an active part in these talks and I expect the Chair to consider my opinions with due diligence and with the respect I deserve." His body language spoke volumes.

Noah Jacobs was not aware of the experience and inner strengths of Ani Shah. She had not obtained her lofty position in the world by being put upon or brow-beaten by any man, even a Senator. Quite to the contrary, he was no match for her. In words that dripped sarcasm and strength, Ani's icy black eyes stared at Jacobs, "Senator, you are just one member of this select committee; saying that, you shall obey the rules of the Chair. Your comments will be accepted and digested but in no way will you dominate

these hearings and discussions. If you feel otherwise, you may leave the room. I, Sir, will run this meeting."

Jacobs responded by casting a cynical look at Ani. He was not used to be treated with sarcasm. On the other hand, Ani was just attempting to regain control of her committee. continued to stand staring at Ani with contempt and rage. For a few seconds the room was still with this impending implosion, then Dr. Robinson raised his voice, "Please forgive me for responding to the honored Senator's comments, but if the Chair will recognize me, I'd like to answer the Senator."

Ani's voice cracked, but she responded, "Of course, Dr. Robinson, you may respond."

"Senator Jacobs, I believe I am speaking for the majority of this committee by saying we must go by the Chair lady's rules. We have critical things to discuss this afternoon. We cannot allow this to become a challenge of personalities; a contest of wills. Please excuse my frankness, Dr. Shah has the perfect right, no, the authority to conduct this meeting as she sees fit. The President has given her that mandate. Senator, please sit and follow the rules of the meeting or leave the room."

Jacobs, realizing that he had been outflanked by one of the most prestigious minds on the planet sat down with a look of embarrassment on his now glowing face. But everyone sitting around the table knew that he was not finished with his interruptions, ideas and plans.

Ani took a deep breath. This was not the way she had hoped this meeting would have started, but she should have realized it knowing the heads-up she had received from Adam. "All right, gentlemen and ladies, now that we seem to have put to bed that little bit of chaos, let's get on with it. What are your comments on the two hundred people split? Let's discuss it further and see if we can get a majority who accepts that principle. If not, we can change the ratios as suggested by our esteemed Senator. The floor is open for ideas, suggestions and comments, but please lets us not get caught in a swamp of infinite details. We may have a dozen more critical topics to resolve." Ani finally was able to exhale and sit back in her chair; the meeting had started.

Once again, Jacobs's hand went up, this time much more subdued. Since there were no other hands showing, Ani responded, graciously, "Yes, Senator, since you have raised your hand to be recognized, may we have your comments?"

"Do you think, Dr. Shah, before we discuss this topic, we should discuss some of the following criteria: age of the people, talents and experience, men or women, child bearing considerations, health. I could go on but you must see my point."

Saul Claussen's hand shot up immediately. "May I answer the Senator, Dr. Shah?" He continued without a response; "Senator, that was the initial criteria that Dr. Shah mentioned to us in choosing our own personal selections. I assume that all of us have made the proper choices on the papers we're submitting for auditing, but we require viewing the overall picture one step at a time. My thinking is to first resolve the numbers game, after which we can weed out the other requirements. Excuse me for speaking out of turn, Dr. Shah." The side-to-side talk and mumbling indicated that the other committee members agreed to his approach to the subject.

"You have not really spoken out of turn, Mr. Claussen," responded Ani. Saul Claussen was the Vice President of the largest steel manufacturing companies on the planet. At the age of 36, he had inherited this responsibility from his father who had founded the company and unfortunately had passed on about five years ago. It was his company that was supplying specialized steel to Davis Engineering. Ani continued, "Although you are perfectly right, Senator, let us go in some degree of order. Your comments are on my notes as business we have to take up in due time."

Once again, Ani felt relief; the rest of the Committee seemed to be following her order of priority.

For the next four hours, almost everyone on the Committee spoke at least twice on their opinions as to the division of the seven- hundred fifty lucky people. Jacobs maintained with some success his suggestions that five hundred-fifty of the savants of the planet be accepted. He received two other additional suggestions when that recommendation was submitted as a motion. Sam Samuels's motion to send fifty elitists was similarly defeated. With growing frustration, Ani listened with patience and respect to the remarks and thoughts of all the members. Finally, at five-thirty, the motion as submitted by Robinson and Ani was passed that there... two- hundred fifty chosen for their unique ability in specific area and five hundred chosen by random methods still maintaining the basic requirements of some talent. Ani, once again sat back in her chair after the vote was counted. "Okay, my friends, we have resolved that issue. However, it is getting late in the day. I have asked our catering people to bring in dinner so we may continue. We must have a list of those initial one hundred people. My secretary and my computer staff are right now compiling those names you have submitted to determine if there is any correlation between them. If there is nothing else to discuss, let's have an hour break for dinner and personal needs. The dining room is down the hall to the right. I'll see you back here at six-thirty."

As everyone rose to take their dinner break, Sue Reynolds's voice rose above the slight dim, "Dr. Shah, before we take a break, may I ask a question not directly related to our discussion but appropriate to the main issue?"

"I don't see why not, Judge Reynolds." Sue Reynolds, a member of the High Court of Zavre was known throughout the planet for her intelligence and down to earth sensibilities and reasoning. She was instrumental, in her years on the bench, in passing many a law protecting the poor and indigent.

As the other members of the Committee returned to their seats, Sue Reynolds continued, "Thank you, Madame Chairperson, for conducting such a difficult meeting with aplomb and directness. But my main question is, can this space ship that you have alluded to carry two- hundred fifty people to another world…another universe? Is this feasible with our limited power sources and technical abilities? Or are we just sitting here playing mind games to satisfy someone's ego, or worse yet keep us out of mischief? Or, as my grandchildren would say, are you pulling my chain?"

Ani thought that she heard someone snicker behind their hand as if in agreement. The room became deadly quiet; the only noise was the ticking of a clock in the outside reception area and one member's breathing problem. Ani had prayed that this question would not arise, but here an individual who would not accept exaggerations or half-truths presented it. The members of the committee leaned forward in their seats, arms on the table waiting for her reply. Even Senator Jacobs was not sure what to expect from Ani.

Ani looked slowly around the room, noting the anxious looks on the faces of the committee members. She fumbled with the neckline on her dress, and turned the ring on her finger to give herself an extra second to compose an answer. She wished, at that moment in time, that Adam Andros were present, but he was not. Finally, with the audience showing a bit of nervousness, she rose from her chair and took a deep breath, "My friends, that is a terribly impossible question. I really wish I had an answer to it, but I don't. I wish I had a full, complete answer to that question. I will not fool any of you if I said I did. I do not know the final answer. All I know is what I told you at the start of this meeting. Dr. Alexia has assured me that various other committees are working on methods for us to leave the planet while others believe they have discovered a destination. Other scientists are finalizing the building of unique power sources that will give us additional power to escape Zavre's gravity fields. Others have been preparing a food supply. For the past five years, all of these groups have been working twenty four hours a day to meet the requirements of inter-space travel and to solve their individual problems. We happen to be the last group. I have great respect for and trust Adam Andros. He is the one who has coordinated all of these programs. It is an impossible job. He and his people are finalizing plans working for seven-hundred fifty of us to escape Zavre prior to it becoming an ice mass and land on another planet. More than this I cannot say. I'm sorry."

Once again the room became quiet; surprisingly no one moved. After what seemed to be an eternity, Noah Jacobs raised his hand, "Dr. Shah, do you have any idea when this plan will go into effect?

Again, Ani took her time to respond, "From my talks with Dr. Andros, he believes that the space ship will have to leave this planet within two weeks to make a rendezvous with an unknown planet that hopefully some of us may be calling home."

Joan Banda, who discovered a seed modification that increased production 50%, finally spoke, "What you are saying, Dr. Shah is that this whole program is a crap shoot. They have no idea if they are going to be successful flying to an unknown planet, which may be hostile and have no environment that we can tolerate. I hope that all of us sitting around this table realize that this trip may take years. This other planet on which we hope to land could be light years away. Wow, I wonder what the odds are that their adventure will be successful?"

"Professor Banda, you are unfortunately right, the odds are not in our favor and the experts who have planned this voyage are aware of this and how far this unknown planet maybe. In their recent calculations, they have discovered that this planet is now much closer than we first believed and this is what we are aiming for. The men and women who have conceived this program have faith; at least they are trying. I know that all of you are aware that within a measurable period of time this planet will be a dead one. The alternatives are not very pleasant."

Robinson interrupted, "Ani, you said two weeks?"

"I'm afraid so, Dr. Robinson." With a low murmur the eleven members of the Committee slowly and quietly left the room.

#

Ani waited until all of the members of her commission left the meeting room before she had the strength to join them in the University dining room. She was exhausted, not physically, but mentally. She felt as if her brain would explode.

The dining room staff, as instructed, had prepared full meals for her guests, including the finest pseudo-meats, fish, salads, desserts and drinks. Although the meal was served buffet style, the serving staff had been instructed to use the best china and silver at their disposal. Ani had previously made sure that her visitors would be treated as honored guests.

But first, as she had promised, she went to her office to call Adam.

Although Jebba had left for the day, Adam was still there and he immediately picked up the phone. "Ani, I've been expecting your call. How did things go?"

"It's better than you said it would be, but worse than I thought. We finally agreed with the number that you suggested after some major discussions ---two-fifty. I will have the two-fifty names later this evening. These will be by talent and ability and the other five-hundred by some lottery system you can propose that still will meet our requirements. If you want to speed up your blast-off date you'll have to work on the lottery program."

"I have already spoken to the Director of the Census Bureau, Ani, about our needs, and he assures me that he can come up with any number of names that will meet our requirements within a few hours. I was waiting for your call to tell him exactly what that number will be. I think I told you, you will have a difficult nasty job."

"You should have been here, Adam."

"I spent many an hour thinking about that, but my being there would have made the discussion too political. I hired you because you have the ability to handle that kind of scenario."

"Adam, the only reason you have me as chairperson as you know I am out of the age requirement to be selected. But, I'll accept your words, you should have been a salesman. That's the best lie I've heard in years." Ani thought she heard Adam laugh on the phone. "I'll get back to you, if not tonight sometime tomorrow with how this all played out. It may not be resolved by tonight, so have patience."

"That's one thing Ani, that I don't have too much of these days. Thanks for the call and the update."

#

Although Ani was hungry from the give and take of the discussions, her stomach was doing flip-flops and she decided, even with her hunger, to partake only in a salad, a small dessert and some water. Zavre only received a restricted amount of water and then intermittently; all the farms could produce was fruits and vegetables that would grow in sandy, ill-irrigated soil.

She immediately noticed that all of her visitors tended to sit together in groups of two or three, depending upon their background and experiences. Ani, on the other hand, took her bowl of mixed greens, drink and dessert to a side table and decided to sit alone. The highly polished wood floor gave off a coldness that Ani felt through her bones and soul.

The cleaning staff had worked through the night to get the room in the best possible condition. It had never been so sparkling clean. Half of the staff had told her privately, they were leaving after this clean-up and would not return. Ani just shook her head and their hands and wished them well. Although she had eaten in this dining room for twenty years this was the first experience she had of feeling its lack of warmth. Even the pictures on the walls of the past Presidents of the University seemed to give off glares of hostility and hatred.

CHAPTER XXIV

Promptly at six-thirty, the eleven members of the Committee slowly entered the meeting area and, with a stillness that indicated their knowledge of the importance of the meeting, took their seats. Ani, standing at the head of the table, was waiting for them.

"Thank you all for coming back on time. I trust you had a decent meal. The University has done its best to meet all your needs and make you comfortable. But to get back to the major thrust of this meeting, for the past thirty minutes, with my computer experts I've been correlating the names of the people you recommended to be considered to board this ship. It is interesting that of the one thousand submitted names, one hundred and sixty were duplicates, an indication that more than one of you have confidence in that person. As we further examined that list, some of the names are duplicated three and four times, a very good sign as to how we respect some of those people's abilities and talents. As I know none of you compared lists prior to giving them to me so there was no collusion. So I can truthfully say these names were given to me without anyone's prior knowledge." Ani's eyes scanned the audience, looking for a dissenting hand.

No one in the small audience raised his or her hand to disagree. Ani concluded that her statement was, indeed, correct.

The room became progressively quieter as they realized what Ani was trying to say to them. She was now getting down to life and death alternatives for friends, relatives and even family. For good reason, there was not a smile in the group. Even Noah Jacobs was aware of the seriousness of this analysis and was sitting forward in his chair. Even he had to think how many recommendations he could have garnered. He glanced about the table and wondered how many of these people even knew of his background and his experiences outside the political game.

To ease her drying throat, Ani took a long gulp from the juice glass that stood before her as she glanced at the Committee's faces. Taking a deep breath, she continued, "If we accept as the finalists for our group only those who have multiple listings we have," she paused as she thought she heard everyone in the room exhale, one hundred sixty people. To repeat myself, these are the people who have been recommended two and three times. To continue this analysis, we now have to consider something that Senator Jacobs had mentioned earlier today, their sex, age, health, occupation and other attributes that may eliminate them from the list. Please recall, at our earlier meeting we decided that these all have the necessary talents. So basically we have to decide on ninety people who meet our criteria from the list of names you have submitted. My friends, I'd like to stop at this point to get, once again, your input as to my overview...is it acceptable by a majority of this group?"

"Senator, let me tell you a brief story of how some of the choosing went. One gentleman was nominated eleven times. A sure candidate for the trip. He is the best electrician and carpenter in the group; a natural. However, in further review, we discovered that he has a bad back and leg and must travel with a cane. Can you all review this passenger in a moving space ship? He, unfortunately was eliminated from contention.

Before she could return to her seat, ten hands went up immediately. Ignoring Jacobs, she accepted Dr. Robinson. "Ani, if my calculations are correct, you're stating that we have to choose ninety people. Would it be improper to obtain the the names of those people still available?"

"Dr. Robinson, I think at this time, the announcement of those names would be a bad idea. In fact, it could be a detriment to the rest of the Committee. After we get down to the lucky two-fifty, then we can disclose the names. I would consider it proper until we get a full complement of two-hundred fifty citizens that we disclose those names and this should be done by our President to avoid problems. Would this plan be acceptable to you? Is there a problem with that?"

Dr. Robinson nodded his head in agreement as all of the Committee indicated their acceptance of that suggestion. The second hand that Ani recognized was from Sam Samuels, "Yes, President Samuels, you have something to add."

"Before we go much further with your excellent analysis Ani, will those individuals meet the basic requirements put down by the esteemed Senator.

"Excellent point, President Samuels, in fact, out of the one thousand names submitted, we had three hundred plus names of individuals recommended multiple times but almost one hundred and forty of those people were eliminated because of advanced age or ill health. This brings us down to the one sixty figure we have to add to."

Jacobs's hand waved violently. "Yes, Senator, you have a point to make?"

"I must ask you this with due deference. You mention that one hundred and forty names were eliminated for various reasons. I would hope that none of those were eliminated because of political reasons or affiliations? And on the other side of the coin, I trust of those approved names, none were recommended because of political pressures?" Those sitting around the table nodded in agreement. This was a question that they knew would be raised eventually, but were afraid to ask. Ani's response was quick and to the point. This was one matter she wanted to squash immediately. She silently prayed that politics was not to rear its ugly head in these discussions.

"You raise an interesting and important point. I assure you with all my heart and soul that none of those people either accepted or rejected were done so because of political reasons. That never has nor ever will become a criterion. I hope, Senator, that answer satisfies your question. Once again, may I ask, if there are any comments on our choice of the one sixty candidates? We still have to choose ninety more citizens to put on board, and I know this will be a heart breaking responsibility."

"Yes, indeed, Ani," Robinson continued, "I fully agree with your concept of the people of choice. Not speaking for the group, I think they are for your elimination concept. However, where do we go from here? How do we decide how to bring the total passengers to seven-fifty? Have you made arrangements to secure five-hundred additional citizens to fill our needs? Do you have a magic technique? We are talking about people's lives here." The ten other members of the committee sat back in their chairs waiting for the ax to fall.

What was the Chairperson going to suggest?

In the next 30 seconds that it took for Ani to verbalize her thoughts, she felt as if she aged ten years. Adam Andros had told her that her job was going to be the most difficult one and, at this moment, she felt the responsibilities of the planet on her shoulders. The lives of many of her co-workers, family, and friends rested upon her next comments.

"My friends, what I say now are only my thoughts. I will ask for a vote on those thoughts. I will give my suggestions to you with no personal attachments involved. I hope that your responses are given in that light. As I stated in my very first phone call, certain basic criteria must be met to meet our needs. Although I trusted that you have done that, I see we have to further tighten up on those requirements. First, we must eliminate, except those with unusual talents and experiences, those who are over an age limit, say... fifty. Second, we require a greater proportion of women over men; third, young families of those selected should be given a preference. Fourth, and this should be a major factor, what are their experiences and backgrounds to enhance their continuing to live on this new planet, and lastly, those chosen most be in good health, not only to survive the trip, but also to survive the rigors of a new world. Using those criteria, we must add more names. It was not my intent to add additional residents from the five-hundred that will be on the magic list. " Ani took a deep breath as she continued, "I must tell you I am in that latter group."

Ani quickly continued before hands for recognition appeared. "Please, ladies and gentlemen, if you want to comment on my suggestions, all well and good. But, please do not nit-pick whether we should consider a fifty-five year old versus a fifty. Or should we reconsider the proportion of women to men from seventy to thirty to eighty to twenty. Let's not quibble over the minor points of my suggestions; let's resolve the meat of the subject. Let's not get bogged down in how sick or incapable someone is or isn't. Let's not waste valuable time arguing over the value of a poet over a painter or a carpenter having more preference than a plumber."

Three of the four raised hands went down immediately. Senator Jacobs' hand remained in the air. "May I, Dr. Shah?" The softness of his voice frightened Ani. *Now he's going to kill me with improper facts and details.*

"From what you recommend Dr. Shah, except for two members of this Committee who are within the parameters you suggest, all others are eliminated." Before Ani could interrupt, Noah Jacobs raised his hands to stop any possible interruption, "This is all well and good as, if I am correct, only I and Mr. Claussen may fall on the good side of the ledger. However, as I once told Dr. Adam Andros, who appointed him God to determine one's life or death and this is just what you are proposing us to do. Although my motion to increase the ratio from two-fifty to five-hundred was defeated, we now see what is occurring; you want this Committee to decide for you this critical issue. I, for one, resent your placing that responsibility on my shoulders. You are forcing me and the other members of this group to play God. A responsibility that Dr. Andros refuses to accept."

Ani sat back on her upholstered chair and gripped the arms so hard that she lost feeling in her hands. She felt her face flush and tears dampen her cheeks. *When she called the eleven members to ask for them to participate, she implied that their decisions would have God-like implications. Why was Jacobs surprised? But what Jacobs was saying was true; she was placing her responsibility on the committee of her choosing to make those life or death decisions. Adam Alexia was correct, to protect his sanity, he had asked her to choose a committee to decide this vital issue. He had chosen her to be the bad guy.*

Before Ani could compose herself and respond to the allegations, Sue Reynolds stood and, with a face as grim and immobile as granite, responded, "Excuse me, Dr. Shah, for taking the floor, but I feel as one of the senior members of this Committee you will allow me to answer the Senator." The ten second pause, that she allowed to escape, only exaggerated the importance of her words. "Senator Jacobs, I am approaching my 83rd birthday. I've spent almost all of my adult years in service to this great planet. I feel honored that Dr. Shah chose me before others to serve on this committee. When she called and explained the mandate she was giving me, I realized the responsibilities I was undertaking. I accepted them knowing that my decisions could mean life or death for millions. I am, Sir, over the age to take this long and dangerous trip and so I will not be on this magical list we are preparing. In fact, we do not even know if the trip will be successful. All we know is that seven-hundred and fifty people will go on a trip to renew a civilization of which we are so proud. I would hope that all of us take that same approach. I would have been happier if we could send 5,000 people on this trip, maybe 10,000. But we would be having this same philosophical discussion no matter what the magic number would be. As Dr. Shah has explained that is logistically impossible and so we have to do what this committee was mandated to do…make these nasty, horrendous decisions. Dr. Shah's work here has shown restraint and a great deal of thought and compassion. She may have been idealistic in some of her views, but someone must lead…and that she has done. To call her or anyone else 'playing God' is unfair and insulting. We have a job to do… let's do it with dignity without throwing barbs in the way." Judge Reynolds gathered her skirt about her and sat down to a smattering of applause.

For a time that seemed like eternity, Ani sat back on her chair, her eyes watering, not knowing how to further respond to Jacobs. If she was not surrounded by eleven others she would have burst into tears by the words so eloquently said by Judge Reynolds. However, she took a deep breath and thought of Adam's words, 'Someone has to do it.'

After a deadly silence in the room, she finally stated, "Just because some members of this committee fall within the criteria we have established, does not mean that their name is included. You must have had at least two or three recommendations. Senator Jacobs, how the other ten members of this committee feel about you and your abilities will be disclosed as we get down to the magic two-hundred fifty number."

Noah Jacobs sat back on his chair, destroyed. He believed that he could re-open the ratio game; he was wrong. He had not previously considered Shah's remarks that he needed to be voted on by his peers. He believed that was a done deal. Now that it was explained, Jacobs was, for the first time, at a loss for words.

Ani raised her hand to get the group's full attention as she continued, "Ladies, gentlemen, if you believe that it is late in the day and you would want to go home to mull over what we have accomplished and still have to complete, I would not be upset. We have discussed and considered a great many ideas and concepts that may have greatly affected our psyche and beliefs. If you would prefer a night's sleep before we continue, let me know."

Almost a full complement of hands was raised at this suggestion. Ani recognized Ambler Socrates, a professor of Philosophy and Sociology at Tova University. She hadn't spoken at all during the meeting, just nodding her head in agreement to all of the comments. "Dr. Shah, although it is late, I think we are progressing slowly but surely in the task that you laid before us and we should continue, regardless of the time. I still believe that some of us still don't get it. On a projection of our geologists and scientists a million of our people will die. If we were to leave, some of us may get second thoughts about the purpose of this meeting and its implications. We may not have the courage to do what we were designated to do."

Ani had to smile at this summary and with a show of hands, the meeting was voted to continue.

For the next two hours, the criteria that Ani had suggested were fine tuned. On the insistence of the Chairperson, everyone took part. Finally, at eleven forty-five, a compromise was reached; two-hundred fifty approved residents would board one of the ships and the other five-hundred would be spread out over the other two ships. The committee finally had its completed list of names.

With shaking hands, Ani handed the list to her secretary for copying and then distribution to the eleven members of her Committee. Without a word, they read the list and without comment left the room. Except for Dr Robinson and President Samuels, no one approached Ani to thank her for her unrewarding job.

President Frisca, because of his age was left off the list. Senator Noah Jacobs, Dr Adam Andros, Eve Maros and Jonah Blanca made the list.

#

The following morning, at eight-thirty, Ani called Adam. He answered within two rings as if he were expecting her call. "Adam, I just finished faxing you the list of two-hundred fifty people that we recommend should go on one of your space ships. I have to tell you I didn't sleep all night. That was the worst job I have ever had to chair. You're a bastard for choosing me."

"Ani, I told you this would not be a job for sissies. If you remember I said, 'Someone gotta do it'. And I felt you had the strength and fortitude to see this thing through. I can't thank you enough."

"I assume I won't be seeing you after this?"

"I guess not. I assume that when I read the list I will know if we were some of the honored few. Although I know this will not be a picnic."

"I guess you'll have to find out like the rest of the lucky ones, the best of luck to you and Eve. Did you get the other five hundred names or will you have to wait?"

"No, I was waiting for your call before I called Falta Fritzi at the Census Bureau. I have to bring both lists to the President this morning and then we're ready to roll. I really wish you were among us."

"C'mon Adam, this trip is made for the young, healthy, and adventurous. Count me out." Ani paused, took a deep breath and then continued, "It's been a pleasure working for you, Dr. Andros. You're a man with vision." She hung up as she broke into tears.

CHAPTER XXV

Six hundred years previously, the United Congress of Zavre, after studying the dynamics of the planet for four years, ascertained that Zavre's future could only exist with a tightly regulated population.

For thousands of years, the population growth of Zavre went uncontrolled. People had unlimited numbers of children and with the advances in medical techniques very few diseases and natural tragedies, the population had swelled without thought or consideration to the long-term implications. During that time, the population of Zavre was 18 million people and growing in leaps and bounds. With Zavre only 15,000 miles in circumference, it was not large enough to support the population growth. It became obvious to geneticists investigating the problem of shortages in raw material, food and water that this was due to the uncontrolled population. With a limited amount of water, the farmers could not grow enough food or raise enough livestock to supply the population. Electric power, although it was almost unlimited, was being used beyond its long-term capability. The huge stands of trees that once covered the planet were almost gone. Even with scientists discovering techniques to make synthetic wood, leather, fibers, clothing, glass, shortages of basic raw material were becoming a fact of life. They had developed chemicals to increase the crop output, lower growth cycles, they had used stem cell technology to increase food production, but with all this new technology the facts became obvious: a more drastic method was required to reduce consumption.

With that knowledge, the Congress realized the obvious; that if the planet was going to exist, something had to be done. The only way they saw this happening was to control, through reasonable means, the population growth. And so within the year chemists started to add a chemical to the water supply that affected both male and female reproduction. The hormone was designed to greatly reduce the sperm count in men, while reducing the egg production in women. Yes, women could become pregnant, but after the first birth there would be a 50:50 chance of miscarrying the second embryo and no chance at a third. Within two years, the average number of children that families on Zavre were having went from five to three. Within the next five years, from three to two. The population was being held under tight control. Major promotion and advertising appeared in the media for the advantages of reducing one's family size.

Within a couple of hundred years, the population of Zavre decreased through natural causes from 18 million to 12 million and then to 8 million. As the generations passed, it continued to decrease and finally within four hundred, it leveled off at two million. By this time very few people knew of the additive being added automatically to the water cisterns. If someone were to ask, "Why are they adding this chemical?" the response by the Water Engineers would have been, "It's for health purposes, it has always been added." No further questions were asked, and as the years went by, no further mention was made on this subject.

With a population set between one and two million, it was easy to monitor who lived on the planet. Four generations ago, numbered identification cards had been issued to every one on Zavre registering them with a central census bureau to monitor their health, schooling, sicknesses, education, jobs, and family background. Everyone on the planet was kept under tabs to prevent inbreeding, but more important to allow them unlimited schooling, if required, unlimited credit, and a source of a mate that would meet their DNA requirements. What had occurred over the past generations was that the intelligence rate of the population had increased almost 15 percent. It was a tightly controlled social environment that may not have been totally democratic, but worked.

With this as a background, it was relatively easy for the Census Director to adhere to Adam's request for one hundred citizens that would meet his specific needs. He tuned up his computer, entered some special software, and within four hours, a list was faxed to Adam's office with the appropriate names.

Adam was amazed. Frankly he, as well as 99.9 % of the population, was unaware of the detailed information to which the Census Group was privy. After reviewing both lists, and noting that there was some duplication in names of individuals already chosen, he called back the Census Group. "I believe there is some duplication in the names you sent me. I need twelve more names. Can you get back to me this morning?"

"I'll give you twelve more lucky souls within the hour, good luck." And within thirty minutes, twelve new candidates were submitted that met all the requirements and were not on any previous list.

As soon as Adam noted that both he and Eve and Jonah were included, he called the President's office and Zak Fellows picked up the phone.

"Hi, Zak, Adam Alexia here, the President wanted me to see him with the final list of those who have been chosen to go on our space adventure."

"Thanks, Adam, he's waiting in his office. Didn't you see him at your early morning get-togethers?"

"No. I've been so busy for the past week that I begged out of those meetings."

"Okay, he's had a real bad couple of days, so make it quick."

“I plan to, Zak, I’m just calling to set up a date to see him. What’s the problem?”

“You didn’t hear the news or see it on the TV?”

“To be honest, no, I’ve been involved with a couple of critical committees to finalize our space trip. Our space window is limited and we have to get all the details in order.”

Adam thought he heard a deep breath from Zak as he came back on the phone, “Chad Asok and his family committed suicide. The President knew Chad and his wife for 35 years. They went to school together and went up the ranks of political offices together. He’s really upset.”

Adam’s hands started to shake. He had heard from the President and through his secretaries and assistants that the suicide rate had gone out of sight, but he didn’t expect it to strike someone so close. “My God, Zak, I’m sorry. He did it before knowing if he’d be on the chosen list?”

“Adam, Chad was no dummy. He knew at his age and with his health problems, he would not be considered. He took what he thought to be the only intelligent way out, as he said in his final note, ‘Excuse me, Mr. President for taking the coward’s way out, but I can’t stand the cold.’ He did have a strange sense of humor.”

The phone was quiet, and then Zak said, “I’m sure that the President will be able to see you at one. Bring Ani Shah; Frisca would like to thank her personally.”

Adam looked at the dead phone for a few seconds, wondering what he should have said to Fellows. What words of comfort could he say to Frisca? It's easy to talk of the planet's demise in the abstract but this was reality. People were killing themselves and neither he nor anyone else could do anything about it. He called Ani, "I hate to re-open this subject, but I am meeting the President at one. He wants you to be there. I have all the names of those who made the final list. He wants to see the names of the lucky ones."

In a voice so low that Adam was not sure if she had heard his request. But finally she answered, "I'll be there."

He then called Eve, "I have to be at the President's house at one. He asked that Ani join me. I have the final list."

Without hesitation, Eve asked, "Did we make it?" Her voice was breathless.

"Yes, we did."

"God, that's great, how about Jonah?"

"He made it. Chad Asok killed himself and his family."

"Oh, my God, I'm so sorry. He didn't even wait for the final list."

"He knew he couldn't make it. I guess the pressure of waiting around for the inevitable was too much."

"Sorry to hear about that. I guess we'll be hearing a lot of that in the next few days. I'm really getting depressed hearing about all of our friends taking their lives. Although I knew this could happen when the news finally got out, when it hits home it's not pleasant." Eve paused for a few seconds to gain her composure, "I'll see you at dinner."

Adam arrived at the Presidential quarters at twelve forty-five. He was taken aback by what he saw. The house was surrounded by double rows of electrified barbed wire fencing and its entrance patrolled by both uniformed police and the military all carrying automatic weapons. He was carefully patted down and two officers with stars on their shoulders examined his identification card. Finally, after a delay of ten minutes, and a phone call, one of the officers said, "Okay, Dr. Andros, the President is waiting for you. Sorry if we delayed you, but you can't be too careful these days. Yesterday, we stopped a man who was carrying a bomb. He was trying to blow up the President. Can you imagine that? Things are getting a bit weird. We had to turn away people who were carrying signs, 'Kill the president!' as if he were responsible for the mess we're in. Are you involved in this space ship thing I've seen on the TV? Your lady friend went in a couple of minutes ago." Adam just ignored the remark and the question and walked up to Frisca's quarters.

Ani stood by the front entrance, a look of sadness on her face. "I guess you also had to go through that security check. It's getting crazy, Adam. The world is losing its grip."

"It's not the world, Ani, it's the people. Are you waiting long?"

"About ten minutes, but I didn't want to walk in without you. You told Eve that the both of you had been chosen?"

"Yes. She was happy that Jonah Blanca was also on the list. Unfortunately, we just heard that Chad Asok took his life. He also took his wife and family. We only knew him a couple of years but he seemed to be a real nice guy. It is, as you said, becoming a real zoo."

After two knocks on the massive oak door, Zak Fellows opened the door. He appeared as if he hadn't slept in days. Without even a polite greeting, he said, "The President is in his sitting room. He's expecting you." He turned and left them.

Adam, knowing the way, walked the short hall to the President's private sitting area, with Ani following. After a slight knock produced no response, Adam opened the door and both he and Ani stepped in. The President was sitting in a side chair. Usually a fastidious man, he was wearing a heavy sports shirt and a pair of well-worn washed-out denims and bedroom slippers. It appeared as if he hadn't shaved in a week. Hair disheveled, his face lined with grief and pain. He stared at the TV showing the town of Tova in flames. Tova, Adam knew, was a small town 200 miles from the Capitol. The TV was showing people running in circles, shots being fired, looting and obvious murder. There was no sign of the police or the militia. It was chaos. The TV reporter was saying that he was going to have to close down the station because of the violence.

Adam and Ani stood by the door entrance, mesmerized by what they were seeing. It appeared to be a violent TV serial they were watching. For a full 30 seconds they were not acknowledged. Finally, President Frisca turned to them and said in a voice that cracked with frustration, "Sorry, guys, I can't believe what is happening. In some of the smaller towns, there are people piled up on the street who have committed suicide. There is no one left to remove and bury them. I guess I shouldn't be surprised for the population to realize what was happening to their world. Please take a seat. This has not been one of my better days. It's a real pleasure to see you again, Dr. Shah. I would have hoped it would be under better conditions. You've done a fantastic job. I would like to say the country cannot thank you enough, but the news is showing otherwise." He smartly shook her hand.

"Thanks, Mr. President, I would have wished that Adam would have chosen someone else. It was an unrewarding and emotional heart wrenching experience, but someone had to do it." She cast an eye at Adam.

Adam took out of his inside jacket pocket the two sheets of paper containing the names of the chosen people. "I guess you'll want to see this?"

Frisca waved the sheets of paper in front of them like a fan, "This was all done on the up-and-up. No manipulation of names for any reason. If my name is here, I'll know there was some foolin' around." He attempted a smile. "Before you arrived, I received a note from Zak Fellows, Ezra Davis did himself in. You'll have to excuse me if I seem not my usual self."

Ani responded very seriously, without a smile, "Mr. President, I'm sorry, we did a lot of work with Ezra and that news is devastating. No, your name is not on the list. Every one on the list was chosen with a purpose. We tried to be as democratic as possible. If there are any loose cannons on board, it was surely not our fault. The Commission that put those names together was beyond reproach. The other five hundred was done strictly by lottery and chance. All they needed was the experience and the talent we believe would be required for a long extended voyage and could make it in another world."

"Are there any women included?"

Ani glanced at Adam for a brief second before answering, "Of course, Mr. President, of the fifty or sixty women that we initially chose, we chose at least twenty who are of child bearing age. We hoped that where we are headed their offspring will survive."

Frisca exhaled a deep breath, "Well, at least I can report that back to the people." He read over the names and then looked up with what appeared to be some dampness in his eye. He wiped his nose with a handkerchief taken from an inside pocket. "Hmm, I see that my son, Bruce, is included.

I hope that is not in deference to me?" He looked at Ani for an explanation.

"Why shouldn't he be included," responded Ani, a little indignantly, "he's a leading authority in farming techniques. As a teacher and an authority on agriculture, if he were not included I would have been disappointed. My God, he wrote four books on growing vegetables in the desert."

The President re-read the list, "I see my other son, Jack, is not included. My wife is not going to be very happy." Ani did not respond. The President rubbed his heavy beard and sighed, "I guess, Adam, you didn't need another attorney in the New World."

"I don't believe we have included any attorneys. These are all working people, people who could be considered pioneers, who can contribute immediately to build a new nation."

"I cannot but notice that your whole team, Eve and Jonah, are included. Would it be upsetting anyone if I asked, "why?"

Ani responded almost immediately, "a good and valid question, you addressed Mr. President. One, we discussed this topic in closed committee for awhile, it was acceptable to the group. Two, Eve is an authority on inter-space travel and living. Two, Jonah is an expert on energy power sources. Without either of them and their leader, she glanced at Adam, we would not have the concept to even get us off the ground."

Frisca shook his head as in agreement, once again glanced at the names, "I note that Noah Jacobs is on the list. I hope you have a good reason for him being there. Knowing him he could have bribed or threatened the Committee."

Both Ani and Adam smiled at the attempt of a joke. Ani responded, "There's something you don't know about our overly aggressive Senator. He's an accomplished and experienced carpenter. In fact, he built his own house. He's a talented guy. Not with people, but with his hands."

"Interesting, I was not aware of that. I guess I shouldn't question the Committee's decisions. Thanks for this information. As far as the list is concerned, I can hardly disagree with any of the names mentioned. The first two-hundred fifty people, some of them I know and they are overqualified. The last five hundred, done by lottery, I would like to believe they were done without prejudice and were chosen with due cause. I shall speak to the people this evening. I will assume you will contact those people on the list. I cannot for the life of me conceive how you put together this list. It must have been an awful job. I gather your special committee were not all happy."

"Mr. President," Ani answered, "for awhile I thought there would be a revolution, but fortunately wiser and calmer heads prevailed and we did what we had to do, although it was no walk in the park."

"When will you notify the recipients of this voyage? Who will inform them?"

"To answer your question, Mr. President, that's all in the works," Adam responded. "We're waiting for your address before we notify the passengers. Within the next two days, they should be gathering at the plant site. There they will then spend another two days learning how to live in a gravity-free atmosphere. We just cannot throw them into outer space without some basic experience," Adam added. He removed from his inner jacket pocket a list of instructions that a doctor knowledgeable in space medicine and Jonah had prepared. "These are some of the instructions that we will include. They are pretty much self-explanatory. I hope that you will give them enough protection so they can get to the meeting place in one piece."

"Adam, I will do my best to insure the safety of these people and inform them of their needs. Once again, thanks for coming in. I guess this will be the last I will be seeing you."

"I'm afraid so, Sir. It has been a real honor working with you. May I ask what are you planning to do for the rest of the population?"

"I will be asking that appropriate companies issue free packets of a sedative for those who want to go that route. We will be putting on TV, other techniques that people may use to do themselves in. I feel awkward in saying this, but someone must take the bull by the horns. I won't comment further on how I feel on that subject. For those of us left, I'm sure the ensuing months and years will not be pleasant, but I'll try to keep some semblance of order. I doubt if I'll be able to prevent the mayhem, looting and destruction that lies ahead. It's a shame that a civilization as sophisticated as this will be overcome by mobs. On a different note, I've been noticing that it's getting noticeably cooler."

"I'm afraid you're right, Sir. The average temperature has decreased another degree. The down slope seems to be increasing. Since our first meeting, almost six years ago, the average temperature has decreased almost ten degrees. The ice flows and glaciers have extended almost 50 miles into the ocean. There are some of our major rivers that are now covered in ice. We must have misjudged when this final disaster would occur. We now calculate that it may occur in less time than we thought. Sorry."

"No need for you to be sorry, Adam, you did the job that I assigned you. I don't know too many people who could have handled the input of information and the personalities as you did, but… that's why we chose you." The President turned away, staring out the window at the wire fences and the mass of people milling on the street and lawn. Some were carrying signs insulting the President, other signs quoting from some religious books.

"I wish I could have done more."

Ani answered, "You did all you could, Mr. President."

He waved off her comment with the back of his hand. "I wonder. Have a good flight. I wish you well." He waved his hand goodbye.

Ani and Adam walked arm in arm out the back exit of the President's house without a word spoken between them. As they reached the exit, Adam asked, "So what are you going to do now? I guess that once the final news gets out, school will be called off and people will just hang out and get drunk?"

"You're asking me a very personal question, Adam. I guess for a couple of days after your space ship leaves Zavre, I'll try to unwind from the strain of what I've been through. I'll finish my bottles of good wine that I've been saving for some special occasion. After that, I suppose, I'll take a long, hot bath and a couple of the pills that will be readily available. I'm not a hero, Adam, and I couldn't stand to see our world just disintegrate into chaos. It's not me." She gave Adam a quick hug and a slight kiss on his cheek, whispering in his ear, "Bless you Adam, may you have many more years." Before he could respond, she spun about and quickly disappeared into the crowd.

#

After Adam and Ani Shah left, Dolf Frisca walked to a small side bar on a far corner wall. There he removed a small glass and a bottle of fine alcohol that had been presented to him by an organization whose name he had long forgotten. He filled the glass and walked to the window watching the milling mobs of people circling the Presidential house with signs and posters screaming obscenities. He slowly sipped the drink and watched the crowd for a few minutes with tears running down his cheeks.

Frisca slowly walked out of his private office to his living quarters. Although he was 62, over the past five years he had aged and appeared as if he were in his late 80's. He shuffled his feet, his shoulders sagged and his face was lined with the hundreds of problems that faced him that had no solution.

In a small, but comfortable living room stood Angi Frisca staring out the window, watching the turmoil and madness that appeared in the streets. Even though the Presidential house was backed 100 feet from the street, the noise and the screams penetrated the room. She looked briefly over her shoulder as her husband entered the darkened room. Although it was just two o'clock in the afternoon, it appeared almost dusk.

"Angi, you should not be sitting in the dark. Can't you put the lights on?"

"Dolf, the electrical people told us last week that they were going to cut back on the service six hours a day, from eight to two."

Dolf just shook his head, remembering that notification.

Angi continued, "I guess the meeting with Andros and Shah didn't go too well?"

"It went fine, they did their job. They gave me the list of those seven-hundred fifty people who are being selected to go on the space ship. Bruce and his family were chosen, not Jack."

"Oh, my God," she screamed, putting her hands over her face. "Do you think that's fair Dolf, selecting one brother over the other? Wouldn't you believe the Committee would have some compassion?"

"Angi, I couldn't conceive how that committee worked out those people. I could never make those choices as to who is selected and who remains. It must have been a terrible experience and I was not going to doubt or question those names or dispute Ani Shah's rationale. I am sure that they must have had a thousand cases in which they had to split families. It was a job I did not want to do. I asked them about experiences they were seeking and Ani did mention that Bruce, being an agricultural expert, was chosen for that reason. The remaining five hundred were chosen by lottery for their talents and abilities."

"It's still not fair, Dolf. Why couldn't they have built another ship to hold more passengers? What was so magic about three? Why not five-thousand passengers not seven-fifty? You should have insisted that both boys and their families be included." She burst into tears.

Dolf took a sip from his wine glass, "Angi, I forced them to use three ships. The initial program was to use only one. I used my authority, which I shouldn't have. Because of that Ezra Davis committed suicide the other day. The guilt is on me. Dolf walked slowly to his wife and took her in his arms as she continued to cry and her tears dampened his shirt front. His only whispered response was, "We didn't have time."

Angi picked her head off his shoulder and looking into his sad eyes said, “What will we do, Dolf, what will we do?”

With his voice cracking, Dolf answered, “Whatever we’ll do, we’ll do it together.

≠

At seven-thirty that evening, Eve had prepared a light dinner in their apartment. Adam and Jonah sat at the ends of the table while she sat in the middle. Knowing the status of the planet and the presence of the final list of those going on this frightening trip, the conversation was in short inane sentences. It was as if no one wanted to talk about anything of any importance.

The phone rang with a loudness that jogged the trio from their own thoughts. Adam picked up the wall phone: it was Ruben James.

“Hi, Adam, you did hear that Ezra committed suicide last night. I am in shock. I really thought he would go the distance. But to carry on, your ships are ready for lift off. We moved them section by section to the blast off area the last few nights and we await your passengers. We have a launch date of next Tuesday at six AM.”

“Hey, that’s great, the President will be talking tonight showing the names of the members who will be making the trip. We’re going to give you two days for their education. These seven-fifty will be at your plant within the next few days for their education. By the way, how come you have it ready so fast?"

"We had every engineer on the planet working on these ships. You realize that two of those ships were seventy percent completed. We just had to change the interiors and the passenger requirements. Normally we'd have one hundred technicians installing the bits and pieces, for this ship we had five hundred. We had so many engineers involved that they were falling over one another. It gave these fellows something to do. We never built anything that big before so it was an adventure and a challenge. I hope you're not complaining. I used every bit of heavy equipment from all over the state in the last two months."

"Hell no, you fellows have done a fantastic job. The President gave the final okay this morning of the list of passengers and we can be sending those seven-fifty to your plant for your short course. Tell them what they should expect and give them the necessary instructions they will require to survive a long trip."

"Adam, it'll take them three days to get them up to speed."

"Ruben you have two---talk fast." Adam hung up and went back to his dessert.

≠

The TV they were watching, while having ice cream, went blank and then came the announcement of the immediate speech by President Frisca. Within seconds, the face of the President appeared on the screen. He was immaculately dressed in a dark blue suit, brilliant white shirt and flaming red tie. His face was closely shaven, his hair neatly cut, and his eyes sparked with energy and enthusiasm. Sitting next to him was Angie, his wife. Adam and Eve just looked at each other. Jonah interrupted the President's introductory remarks, "I guess he has to finally say what he has to say. I feel sorry for him." Adam and Eve both nodded as they heard the President's words flow from his lips.

Frisca spoke with his usual eloquence, calmness and yet some sadness. He explained the reason for the final decision by the scientists to leave the planet. He spoke of the formation of an Ethical Commission to decide who should leave Zavre. He discussed their requirements; emphasized that those on the ship were chosen by majority vote of the Commission and then by lottery. He briefly touched upon the fact that one of his sons was chosen, while a second would remain. He explained that within the day all those on the list would be notified to go to the assembly plant to get prepared for the proposed voyage. Their names would appear on the TV after his remarks. They also would be contacted by phone. He hoped that their trip to the space ship would be done in an orderly manner. He stated briefly how dangerous and long the trip would be. He glanced at his wife three or four times and held her hand. He concluded by thanking all those committees who worked so long and hard on their respective responsibilities and especially to Dr. Adam Andros who coordinated all the committees. The President finished by saying, "God bless all of you on Zavre and God speed to our travelers may their voyage be successful."

It would be his final speech. It lasted, according to Jonah's watch, slightly less than nine minutes. After Frisca words, for three minutes the screen showed in large capital letters, seven-hundred forty two names. Eight previously accepted citizens had changed their minds and choose instead to remain with their families. It then went blank and then was followed by the words, "THIS STATION WILL BE CLOSED INDEFINATELY DUE TO CONDITIONS BEYOND IT'S CONTROL"

CHAPTER XXVI

Eve broke the silence in the room, "Jonah, are you packed? I hope you only take a change of clothing and a couple of changes of underwear."

"If I knew you were just joking, I'd laugh, but I know this is serious stuff. What happens if it's cold where we're goin'? Don't you think I should bring a warm coat?

"Please don't. Number one, you complained about the extra weight and two, they must have a warm zone. I believe the planet shares our sun without the mist."

Adam stretched his arms above his head, "Is there anything that I should know about what has occurred while I was taking care of the administrative part of this deal?" He looked at Eve and Jonah.

Eve finished her beverage and answered, "If you must know, Adam, while you were involved with the President and Shah, I convinced Ruben James at Davis Engineering to install a small version of my radio laser telescope. I can hook this up to my computer and know what's ahead of us. It'll be on a rotational device that I can turn 360 degrees. It should be of major help to our pilots.

"It's a much smaller version of the one I have in the observatory. If it works, it'll be a great help, if it doesn't, at least we tried."

The three sat quietly in their chairs. Adam finally remarked, "Jonah, you've been in contact with our pilot, Yari Roebling and his two buddies?"

"Yes, I've been talking every few days with Yari and his two assistant since our meeting with Davis who told him the whole story. They thought we were out of our minds but was willing to take on the challenge. They figured they had nothing to lose. All three have no family and this project would keep them busy for awhile. They have been attending classes to fly this ship for the past month and what to possibly expect. My gut feeling is that Yari is a good man and from what I have heard a damn good pilot. He'll be the oldest man on board at fifty-seven. I'll be the co-pilot, as I have to control the power sources. It could be quite a learning experience. He'll be on our ship and each of his friends will be on the other ships. We'll be in touch via phone so we can coordinate controls and directions. They are equally good pilots so we should be in capable hands."

"Is there anything else that we should know about?" asked Eve.

"There is quite a bit that you're not aware of."

"Really," Adam said, looking over his glass of wine. It was an answer he was not expecting.

"Well, while you were gabbing with Ani Shah and Noah Jacobs and our President, I was in deep conversation with Ruben James and William Able. They came up with some innovative ideas that we will use."

"Okay," said Adam, "surprise me with your new ideas. I thought I was the Project Director."

"Of course you are and will be, but there are issues that you were not aware of that we had to resolve immediately. I believe, after you hear me out, that Loren and Ables' thoughts have increased our chances of making this trip a successful one."

"Let him finish, Adam, and don't be so high and mighty!" Eve said loudly.

"As usual, you are right, fire away, Dr. Blanca." Jonah gave Adam a dirty look. "Okay, this is the situation. First, when we get above five to ten thousand feet we will not have sufficient oxygen; the cabin will have to be pressurized. Oxygen will be pumped into the face masks for breathing. However, at appropriate times, that oxygen will also contain a sleeping gas. This will put our passengers in a never-never world and to sleep. What will occur is that when they awaken from what they think was a short nap, four days will have passed.

Understand? When they awake they will be hungry as wolves, but you win some and you lose some."

Adam interrupted, "Could you keep them on this gas forever?"

"Sorry, no. Too much of this gas could affect their lungs so we will have to stop the gas every two or three days and pump in oxygen to clear their system. After breathing good stuff for a week or two, they should be okay. They will never realize what was going on. You have to remember that this trip may very well awhile. You remember that the planet we are shooting for hopefully will be a light years away; that's not around the corner. However tough these people may be, they can go out of their minds with boredom. On the same subject, we will be telling the passengers to drink a pint of our liquid supplement. Abba Able told me they will be hungry as wolves, and I have to agree, that we should include in that liquid a small amount of a tranquilizer to keep the people happy or to be honest, slightly sedated."

Before Jonah could continue, Adam said, "My God, Jonah, do you think that is really necessary, these people will be zombies."

"Adam, let's be realistic, being in an atmosphere of weightlessness for years can drive some of these people daft. It was a great thought, I believe. They tried both ideas on some laboratory mice and it worked.

Eve looked at Adam with amazement. Adam appeared tongue tied, finally Eve asked, "Will this include us?"

"I hope not. When required we will also be wearing face masks. You can regulate the oxygen or gas intake. I will need you to refill the water bottles or to show the people how to walk in a gravity-free atmosphere. You, Eve, can keep our pilot on course with your new device."

"Are there any other brilliant things that I should know?"

Jonah looked sheepishly at his friends, "There's one other thing we overlooked and I was reminded of this by Able's medical staff. They off- handedly mentioned that if the passengers are going to be in space for an extended time, they would lose their minerals, calcium mostly, which would make their bones weak. He suggested that they incorporate into their magic liquid 400 milligrams of calcium; that should solve that issue. It's really not enough calcium, but it's the best they could do in the time frame they had."

Adam sat back in his chair and finished the last of his ice cream, "I gotta give you credit, you have thought of things that I could not have conceived. What ya think, Eve?"

"You're one special guy, Jonah. What the hell would we do without you?"

"Thanks Eve, let's drink to that."

That was to be their last drink on Zavre.

CHAPTER XXVII

Adam was in his office at seven-thirty the following morning trying to tie up some loose ends. He knew in his heart that there were things that he overlooked, people to whom he had not said goodbye, options he could have taken but because of the stresses of the years could not accomplish. Sitting with his head in his hands he thought about Jebba, his secretary for almost fifteen years who was leaving him the following day.

How could he keep her even another day when she explained she wanted to be with her parents and family for the final days? All he did was hold her in his arms and let her tears flow. He was devastated. The people that he had consigned to remain on Zavre were non-entities, people with no faces, but Jebba was like family. Her leaving was a wake-up call to what was really happening on Zavre.

He heard the phone ringing in the outer office and Jebba picking it up and saying her hello. It could not have been Eve, she was in the shower at this time. Jonah probably was fine tuning his new energy producing batteries now being installed on the vehicles. He was such a fanatic and obsessive compulsive; he would never be satisfied with what he had accomplished unless they were perfect.

Jebba's face appeared in his office door, "Dr. Andros, the call is someone who claims he's your brother, a Mr. Crees Alexia. If he is some kind of a nut only calling to insult you, I'll hang up. What do you think?"

"My God," Adam said out loud, "that's my brother, I haven't heard from him in years, please put him on." When their mom was alive they would get together on some major holidays two or three times a year but since their parent's departure they hadn't been in touch.

Adam picked up the phone and he immediately recognized the voice. "Crees, how are you? We haven't spoken since Mom passed away almost ten years ago. How are you and your family?"

Speaking in a low, worn- out tone, Crees replied, "I've been reading a lot about you and realize that we didn't have too much in common these days. I took over Mom and Dad's farm after his passing. I have a wife and two children and things were going along rather well until this misting situation took over almost six years ago. Planting became a joke as the fields, without the heat of the sun, couldn't produce any crops. For the last two years I've been working as a machine mechanic fixing farm equipment. It's not very lucrative, but I made a decent wage. The kids must have had your genes as they passed all their exams with flying colors and have been accepted in the local university. It's quite ironic that the kids have been working their butts off to get into school and now this. But from what we have heard from the President, that's all going down the drain. I gather what Frisca said was the truth."

All Adam could answer was, "What Frisca described was unfortunately the truth. We have been working for almost six years trying to put together a space vessel to get us off this planet before it is covered by ice. There is no other alternative. I'm terribly sorry Crees, I wish I could do something for you and your family."

"You don't have to be sorry, Adam, you were always the lucky one in the family. Tonight, our family and our neighbors will be having our farewell party and I wanted to say goodbye."

"Farewell party?"

"What the neighboring families have been doing is that they invite four or five families to a big get- together. Every family brings their specialty dish and then after dinner they serve an after- dinner drink containing some drug…got my drift. Within an hour they are all gone. We feel that is the best way to go. Waiting to freeze to death doesn't sound too inviting. We plan to do this tonight. We will hold hands with our kids and say goodbye to this great world of ours."

Adam took a deep breath before he could respond. For the first time in years tears rolled down his cheeks. He was at a loss for words. He responded with the only words that he could think of at the time, "Crees, my best to you and the family. We will see you in another world."

Crees response was poetic, "Have a good trip with Eve. We will meet again."

CHAPTER XXVIII

Three days later, at two- thirty in the morning, ten buses, surrounded by an army of soldiers for protection, brought seven-hundred thirty travelers and their personal possessions to the launch pad site. To insure safety of the passengers, armed guards had escorted the vehicles. Even then, there were a few incidents that caused some concern. One, bottles filled with flammable liquids were thrown at the buses, which, luckily, missed their targets. The second, which caused an hour's delay, was the piling of debris on the roadway that forced the convoy to use a roundabout route. Fortunately, the buses arrived safely, albeit late. Jonah, Adam, and Eve could not understand what these people were trying to accomplish. Adam summed it all, "When people are frustrated and have no hope, they do foolish things."

Twenty eight potential passengers changed their minds the last minutes...to the utter annoyance of Adam. They had spent the preceding two days in Ruben James's manufacturing plant learning how to survive in space. His engineers had walked them through the ship showing them where to hold onto the supports when in a weightless atmosphere. They tried to emphasize the need to be kept busy when not sleeping. They put all the vital information in a short handbook which was given to all of the passengers.

Jonah had hoped for a mid-night departure that, he believed, would do well in his upcoming time/energy calculations chart. He would have to adjust his figures accordingly. Roebling, on the other hand, was aiming for the right moment when Zavre's rotation positioned itself for the most direct path to its window. Roebling would also have to amend his flight plan slightly.

As soon as the passengers put away their possessions and got comfortable in their assigned recliners, Jonah shut off the cabin's soft music, lifted the microphone and started his prepared speech:

"Friends, I'm Jonah Blanca, co-pilot on this plane. I am one of the researches who developed the batteries that will give us the power to escape the gravity of Zavre. This ship was especially designed and built to take you into outer space and to a new world. Our pilot is Yari Roebling, a world-renowned test pilot and the most experienced pilot on Zavre. I can assure you, you're in good hands. Before our pilot uses our rear reactors to blast us off this planet and then into the blue, let me alert you to the following. Although I know for the past two days you have received instructions, it's worthwhile to repeat some of what's goin' to happen. Some of what I'll tell you may even be new to you.

"One, once we take off and gain some altitude, compressed air will automatically be pumped into the cabin. This will allow you to breathe normally. At the heights we will be flying, oxygen will be present but too thin for us to live. All of you have been issued face masks which will allow you to breath normally. A few of us will be using special oxygen masks. This will allow us to get around better and do our job so do not fear.

"Two, in the seats in front of you are self-contained oxygen masks that we will ask you to put on as we land on our unknown planet. We believe that the air there will be acceptable, but a little caution is always good. Three, in the compartment above your seats are enclosed shelves containing enhanced liquid food supplements. We have planned that we have a sufficient number of these baggies to last for the length of our trip. We suggest the first time you get hungry take two, it will react faster. Drink plenty of water initially. Afterwards drink normally. Do not waste it, as you will require all you have when we re-enter our new planet's atmosphere. We will have to recycle the water so don't be surprised if the water has some flat taste. It will have been filtered and chemically treated. It will have to do. You will require it when the ship goes into a re-entry mode and the ship starts to heat up. It will get warm within the cabin.

"Four, once we get out of the force of gravity, we will become weightless; this means that if you are not tied or strapped down you will float about like helium balloons. Please keep all your personal possessions secured, otherwise things will be floating all over and may possibly cause damage. This is important. If you were wondering, this is why we have those holders on the ceilings and the floors; they are for you to hold on to when you move about the cabin. You've all been instructed as to how to handle weightlessness in the two days of classes you attended. I hope you remember what to do.

"Five, and most important, this trip may take years. We believe that the planet we are aiming for will be moving toward us, which may shorten our trip. Furthermore, by using unique batteries designed by our research people, we hope to shorten this trip. Our space experts claim it still will take years, that is the best we can hope for. I know it will be difficult and boring. We have placed in compartments, just before the bathrooms, music for you to hear, books for you to read and other games with which to entertain yourself during this long voyage. Have patience with yourself and with the other passengers. Remember, they are in the same boat as you. Just remember within a very short period of time there will be no life left on Zavre."

Senator Jacobs raised his hand cautiously, "Excuse me, Dr. Blanca, I understand almost everything that you say, but what about bathroom facilities. If we're goin' to be stuck on this craft for as long as you believe, you must have made provisions for the obvious."

"Senator, all that information is in the instruction booklet you received and the classes you took. But to answer, the bathrooms are under compressed air so that any bodily functions can be accomplished normally. Once you close the lid of the commode and press the discharge button, it automatically will discharge your waste by compressed air into outer space. It's the best we could do under the situation. Remember to close the lid before you press the discharge button, otherwise, you'll be splattered." The rest of the passengers laughed. It was a question that had to be answered.

Jacobs continued with his question, "Thanks for that answer, Jonah, but you also mention that this trip may take years. Can you be a little more specific?"

"Once again, Senator Jacobs, at this time we don't know the exact time it will take. That is dependent upon how fast we travel. Our experts believe that we may be able to reach a speed of 17,000 miles an hour. We may even be pushed faster by galactic winds. Who knows? But even then expect this trip to take a number of years. This is why it was so important that our new battery system be installed. After we get going, I'm sure our pilot will let you all know." Jacobs sat back in his recliner, seemingly satisfied with that vague answer.

"If there are no further questions, I'll put the cabin music back on; ask you to make sure your masks are on tight and ask our pilot to go to work."

It had been a little less than six years since Adam had received that phone call from the President on that Saturday morning.

CHAPTER XXIX

And this is how it happened in the year 10,253 at four-thirty in the morning that the space ship blasted off the surface of Zavre. With almost five thousand people surrounding the blast off site, some throwing objects at the ship, some coursing, others on their knees praying while others huddled together in tight bundles.

With Yari Roebling in the pilot's chair of the lead ship and the co-pilot Jonah Blanca with Eve sitting behind them handling the directional instruments as the last of the two-hundred forty two passengers snapped on their face masks, Jonah pressed the eight battery reactors, he had developed, to lift the ship off its cradle. The two other ships, already loaded with their passengers were waiting for words from Yari and they would follow his direction.

And so into the black void of the universe the huge space ship blasted off its gurneys its speed gradually increased. Within two minutes, as it approached ten miles above the surface of Zavre, it was traveling almost 2,500 miles per hour. At that time, Yari Roebling put on all the power that the normal rear reactors battery could muster. The 550-ton plane instantly jumped ahead to a speed of 5,000 miles per hour.

At fifty miles gaining altitude and speed rapidly, Yari signaled to Jonah, "Jonah, you're sure you want me to continue this. I can still bring this bird back to Zavre."

"Yari, this is not the time to ask. We've discussed what we planned to do, do what you have to. Do it!"

"Okay, but after you feel the release, the ship will need additional thrust to obtain escape velocity. I was led to believe that at 200 or 250 miles we escape gravitational forces and become weightless. " He then blew off the rear reactors of the spacecraft so they flew without any additional drag.

Jonah, who had installed 36 of his latest batteries on the ship, waited for the release of the booster rockets, then set off six batteries, three from each side of the craft. He would save the remaining for a later time. The ship's burst in power was immediately discernible and the huge vessel instantly shot up to 200 miles at a speed of 11,000 feet per second. As the ship raced towards the sun, Yari said to Jonah, "You sure you know what you're doing? If we get too close to the sun we'll be drawn into its gravity sphere and be burned up. I hope this is not your plan?"

"I'm afraid that's the only way we can get enough speed to get where we want. You take us twice around the sun after which the sun's extra push, some strong solar winds and my shot of power from my new batteries should push us up and away. You released the first stage of the ship which will make us lighter and easier for my batteries."

Yari looked at Jonah with a quizzical look, "I was not happy with this flight plan when you first proposed it to me and I still think it's crazy, but let's hope it works."

"You're the pilot, Yari, let's make it work." Yari took the space ship around the edges of the sun's gravity once and silently prayed. Within ten minutes they were traveling with the aid of Jonah's energy boosters, at super-sonic speed.

Much to Jonah's surprise, the scenario as described by Adam, almost six years previously, with his story about a sling shot theory, worked to perfection.

"Yari, Adam asked after the first trip, "how are your friends doin'?"

Yari just smiled, "they're right behind us. I taught them well."

After the second spin of the ship about the sun, gradually picking up speed, Jonah set off six more of his boosters. The ship flew into outer space at a speed of 10,000 miles per hour. It had ceased to become a space ship, or a missile but a glider. With no gravity constraints to hinder its forward motion, the craft continued to pick up speed dramatically.

Jonah floated toward the back of the craft. Not unexpectedly, all of the passengers were strapped in their seats, with their face masks in place, he hoped, for a blissful, long nap. He noticed that Eve was not wearing her face mask and was in a deep sleep. Adam, on the other hand, removed his mask for a second and whispered, "I guess that stupid plan of mine worked."

"Don't tell me at this date you had questions?"

Adam just put his face mask back on and smiled underneath it.

≠

Six days later with the spacecraft traveling at super sonic speed and more than 7,500 miles an hour and more than a million miles into their journey, Jonah shut off the supply of gas to the passengers. Within an hour all of them were alert, a little groggy, but able to ask, "How we doin'…I'm starved."

"Have another drink," Jonah repeatedly answered, "we're doin' great." As he was going to climb back into his recliner one of the men approached him. "Excuse me, Dr. Blanca, I am Dr. Ira Andretti. May I have a moment of your time?"

"Of course." Adam, Jonah, Eve and Yari Roebling gathered to hear the comments.

"Gentlemen, Dr. Masos, I am one of two doctors on this adventure, and I realize what you are doing with the air delivery system. Once you smell that sweet gas you never forget it and I've had a great deal of experience with that gas. I cannot fault your use of this item, as it surely will decrease the wake time of all of our passengers. However, please be aware that if we are going to have that many years of weightlessness, and then sleeping, we will develop atrophy of our limbs. If we do not exercise those legs and arms we will lose all the strength in them. It could be tragic." He glanced at the four with a look that indicated that he knew what he was talking about.

"Does the other doctor know of this situation?" asked Adam.

"The other doctor, Dr. Franklin, is an animal doctor, a veterinarian; he knows nothing about temporary anesthesia."

It was silent in the group, this is something they had not thought about, and then Adam spoke, "Doctor, to be quite frank, we had never considered that potential problem and as you describe it, you are perfectly correct. As a doctor what would you recommend?" The others agreed by shaking their heads.

"I would suggest, very simply, that every time they come out of their sleep they go into an exercise program. I could put together a simple series of exercises that should do the trick. All I would need is your approval and some room to do this."

Jonah answered, "That's a great idea. Of course you have our approval. We will set up an exercise routine in which you can have twenty passengers at a time for a half hour for calisthenics. Would that be okay?"

"Perfect."

"Good, I'll announce the program and prepare a schedule to get everyone involved. Yari, contact your friends in the other ships for them to prepare a similar program."

They all agreed.

≠

The following month, as Jonah moved about the great cabin, Eve motioned him over. "What's going on, Eve?" She had her computer on her lap and, using Jonah's new batteries, was able to keep it in service. She was perpetually examining the skies via her radio laser waves looking for the destined planet and to ascertain the proper direction.

"I have some great news. One, I've been following the track of the plane and we're right on course. The ship's guidance system seems to be working perfectly. Roebling is headed for the right quadrant. You guys couldn't have chosen a better pilot. Interestingly enough this planet is a relatively new one just traveling in space looking to get into the proper orbit about the sun.

"Interesting, as far as I can make out, it seems to be coming out to greet us." She smiled as if she had just won the lottery.

"You're kiddin' me," said Adam as he and Jonah both looked at the screen on her computer. Neither of them could read its strange numbers and figures.

"What are you talking about, Eve; you were so sure that the planet we were seeking was at least two light years away."

"Well, fire me," answered Eve, "according to my latest calculations, it is less than a light year away and it's in an orbit that seems to be moving closer to us. For some reason it seems to be spinning our way. Not too bad, just a hop, skip and jump as the astro- physicists would say. It's still a light year away so don't expect a rendezvous next week."

"Well, Jonah, do you think we'll get to this place before our hundredth birthday?"

"I wish I could answer that Adam, we're moving along at a fast clip, but we'll see. Let's hope for the best."

Two months later, Jonah, making his daily inspection of the ship to make sure that the water supply was adequate and everyone was taking their energy liquid, discovered four people had expired.

When he brought the news back to Adam, he exclaimed, "God, what the hell's goin' on here? I thought your committee chose people in good health?"

"Jonah, I wish I had the answer to that. I guess some people lied about their health while others just couldn't take the strain of weightlessness and boredom. I guess we'll be having more of that as we continue."

Fifteen minutes later, Yari joined them in their small office, "I just spoke to my friends in the other ships. Yonni told me they lost sixteen potential voyages. Jacki, in the third ship did not want to give me his exact number, just saying we may end up with less than seven-hundred total passengers. I guess we will have more of this however frustrating it is."

CHAPTER XXX

For another two years, Archangel, the space ship, raced through space. Alternating solar winds, which they hadn't expected, had boosted their speeds considerably. Unfortunately, once or twice a week, Jonah found a man or women in his or her final sleep. Dr. Andretti examined them briefly and said, "Their hearts just gave out." All Jonah could do was shrug his shoulders; *this was the price of survival.*

And then just after their second year into the flight, Eve approached Yari Roebling. "Yari, I just picked up a massive intergalactic explosion that is right behind us. It should reach us shortly. It seems a planet has just exploded, and we will be hit with its shock waves. Those waves are traveling close to the speed of light. The one good feature is that it will further push us toward our target and faster."

Yari interrupted before she could continue, "You mean as long as we don't get torn apart."

"Yari, Ezra Davis at Davis Engineering, assured Jonah that they used the very latest metal technology. This ship should hold up to almost any condition. We've come all this way, don't be a pessimist. Shall I wake Jonah and Adam?"

"I guess we should let the Boss know what to expect. We also have to wake and alert the passengers, they've been sleeping on and off for the past month. I'll just keep on course and hold onto this stick a little tighter; things could get a little bumpy."

"I think ya better. I'm goin' to stop the flow of gas. I'll tell Jonah and Adam, and the rest of the passengers to expect some disturbance and try to stay in their seats for the next few days."

As Eve was preparing to lift the speakerphone, Yari stopped her,"Eve, can you tell if that explosion was from Zavre? Could our old home have blown up?"

With a sorrowful look on her face, Eve answered, "It's coming in the direction of Zavre so I assume it's our old planet. I guess our more religious people would say, 'they are now among the Gods.'" She reached to close off the gas supply.

Yari nodded and added as he went back to his consoles, "Some mighty good people have now joined their ancestors." Eve just nodded.

Two days later, with all the passengers fully awake, belted in, and alerted to the imminent shock waves, the craft was hit by a huge hurricane force wind that lifted Archangel and literally threw it forward. The huge ship, almost 550 tons, was tossed about like a matchstick in a tornado. For thirty seconds, the rocket was lit with an unusual brilliance that almost blinded all the travelers, even though the shades of their windows were drawn. And then, as suddenly as it had started, it passed. The spaceship became quiet and still and, thankfully, remained all in one piece. If they had not been prepared, there could have been major damage. That blast and windstorm threw the ship almost 500,000 miles further toward their destination. It was as if the departed citizens of Zavre were saying, "Here is a present, go with additional speed." That being said, six passengers died from shock and heart failure from the violent turbulence.

Adam and Jonah sat belted in their seats and reflected on what had just occurred. Without saying a word, they both realized how close they had come to being destroyed. If they had been closer to their old planet, the shock waves would have torn their spacecraft apart, but being two years out allowed them to escape all of its pent up fury. Both men had expected some type of a galactic explosion when the cold and ice reached the inner heat confines of the planet. This had occurred sooner than they had anticipated but it was to be expected. Fortunately, except for Eve, no one on board realized his or her good luck.

Jonah looked sadly at Adam, "I guess this is the last we will see of old Zavre?"

"You're right, my man, it just went by us."

For two more years, time went by without too many incidents. A few disagreements and arguments over possession of reading material and words were exchanged, but all in all the passengers conducted themselves with patience. Jonah explained this by saying, "The addition of the trace amounts of sedatives in the tablets led to their laid back attitudes."

Unexpectedly, twelve more passengers passed on from various ailments. Fortunately, none of the deaths were caused by a viral or bacterial ailment which could not be treated on the space ship. It was a depressing time for Jonah and Adam to remove the bodies and send them into outer space via the ship's compressed air system. Adam continually wondered if he should have anticipated this problem and had given Ani Shah more information. His only self response was he could not think of every possible problem.

Roebling or the doctor said a few words over the remains and then Adam pressed the release button and the body disappeared into space. Although both Adam and Jonah expected some deaths on the long trip, it cast a spell of depression on those remaining members.

The following month, Jonah found twelve more passengers unconscious. He called Dr. Andretti, "Doc, what the hell's goin' on here?"

Andretti examined the bodies with a perplexed look on his face. "Jonah, I hate to tell you this but it seems that these folks are dying from an unknown virus. Without extensive blood tests, I can't determine exactly the type or how to prevent this from continuing."

"But what is it from, Doc?"

"Jonah, my only guess is that we are recirculating the air in the cabin and although the carbon dioxide scrubbers are doing their job, a virus of some type must have entered the cabin and people who have weakened immune systems are passing away. This is my only thought. I wish I had a better answer for you."

"Will this continue," asked Jonah?

"It very well may. We better get to where we're going rather quickly for a supply of fresh air or the weakest among us will be victims."

"Is there anything that you can suggest?"

"Pray."

#

The music that Jonah had piped into the ship during its early days had been stopped a long time ago. Some people claimed that hearing the same music over and over was making them neurotic. Adam could not disagree. Needless to say, the books that Eve had brought on board had become, by this time, worn and in shreds. The decks of cards were worn to a pulp and the board games had lost all their flavor and excitement. Life was becoming a horrible, boring event and Jonah was incorporating more nitrous into the system than he had planned. Even then, the two or three days that the passengers needed to be awake to rejuvenate their lungs and to exercise were becoming an effort and the deaths slowly added up. Not knowing if it was night or day added to the confusion. It became apparent, even to a non-doctor as Adam, that some of the people were becoming psychotic: their inner clock was completely out of whack. All Andretti could suggest is that they keep the worst cases under sedation. He did not want to repeat the virus specter.

Jonah or Adam replaced Roebling every other day as pilot to relieve him of the strain of maintaining the proper course. At least during that part of the voyage, it was a simple task, using a gyroscope, with Eve's directions and the built in guidance system; the ship stayed on target, although they all had to admit that the target could have been shifting as they flew toward it.

Finally, a year later later, Eve, maintaining her position as scout for the voyage, screamed, "That's it, that's it!" She spun away from her computer screen and pulled the two men toward her. Roebling was taking his deep, well deserved, nap. "I see the planet we are headed for. Interesting it has a moon circling it. It's about four months from here. The only thing I could say is please remind Yari that at the speed we're moving we'll need some time to slow down for a landing. Otherwise we'll fly right by our destination. I'll keep you up-to-date on that score, although Yari should be aware of that potential problem. Right now he's on target.

"I suggest Adam or Jonah talk to the folks about what's going to happen with the heat and so forth. Sound like a reasonable thing to do?"

When Yari woke the following day, after his mandatory sleep, Adam told him of Eve's discovery and suggestions. "Eve was perfectly correct," he replied, "we have to drop to an altitude of about 500,000 miles from the planet. We'll still be going at excess speeds, and there is no air at that height for me to control this ship. We'll have to drop to 50,000 miles until I can control some of the braking devices. I'll start to slowly put the brakes in motion. That should slow the ship but not nearly enough to get us to a controllable speed. We will still be going so fast that this bird will begin to really heat up as it smashes into the air molecules faster than they can get out of the way. We'll be going so fast that we'll actually knock the electrons off some of the molecules, creating an ionized gas cloud that will shut off all of our electrical power. When I get to 200,000 miles from the spot that Eve says I should drop down, I'll throw my brakes on full; that should slow this ship down further. I hope that at that speed the brakes and the landing devices will not be torn off. When I'm at 50,000 miles from the drop spot, we'll still be doing 500 miles per hour. At that time I'll need Jonah's batteries to give us additional braking power and just hope for the best."

"How do you know all of this, Yari?"

"For a month I was having daily eighteen hour meetings with various aeronautical engineers and pilots discussing this re-entry problem; I've been going through practice maneuvers and the like. We practiced on some hypothetical conditions and scenarios, you guys have had it easy. I've been working my tail off 18 hours a day to learn this stuff. To be honest, it's all new to me. What I have just explained to you is all theoretical. The speeds and the distances that I gave you are strictly guesses so don't hold me to them. No pilot on Zavre ever experienced what we're going to go through. I hope they knew what they were talking about."

Yari continued, "As soon as possible, I will start decreasing our speed if we are to land at 140-160 miles per hour. If we come in too much faster than that we'll tear apart. This baby was designed to land at 140 miles per hour; more than that I don't know how it will handle. Jonah, I hope those remaining batteries of yours can help us slow down."

"That's what I have saved them for. I have them faced forward so they can act as brakes. How efficient they are, we'll soon see. But I'm amazed that we got here so fast. I would have thought it would have taken us another two years."

"Yari, talk to your pilots, see if they know what's goin' on."

"I already have. Their navigators have already planned their landing. Didn't I tell ya I trained them well?"

"I hope your right, Yari, I wouldn't want to lose a ship with its travelers. But a lot of things have been happening while you were snoozing. One, we have been traveling at speeds not considered by the aeronautical expects back on old Zavre. Second, we have been pushed forward by some major wind storms and third, the planet that we were seeking is coming to meet us. According to Eve, the planet is at the short end of its eclipsical swing. We will get the short end. This will save us almost a light year in distance. Without discussing some other theoretical stuff, let's say we have been lucky. Now if we can continue our luck and start to slow this ship down before we over-shoot our target we may be real lucky. Of course hitting a good landing area would not hurt but, I'll leave that up to Eve. She seems to have the magic touch for finding things."

"Are you sure you can do this, Eve?" asked Jonah.

"I'll be doing my best, Jonah, but to be honest, this is all theoretical; perhaps someone in the future could tie together the relationship between space and time. Secondly, we've traveled over a light year. That means we've gone over six trillion miles. Eight point three trillion miles, to be exact, and in that time the planet that we've been aiming at has been in its own cycle. Fortunately we may be catching it when it is closest to us. It's amazing. We've been very lucky. Now if we can continue our luck and the engineers who designed this ship have placed sufficient heat shields so that we don't burn up, we'll be in good shape. We then have to slow down enough so that we don't scoot by our possible landing area. This is goin' to be tricky."

Adam concluded the short meeting, "I'll talk to the passengers. Yari, do what you have to; remembering to confirm our position with Eve, otherwise we'll come in like a bullet rather than a glider. After all this time, I'd like to make some type of a reasonable landing. Jonah, can you replace the gas with pure oxygen so I can talk to the people and you can coordinate your battery brakes with Yari?"

"Of course, Adam, but it'll take a day for them to completely wake up." Two days later, Adam addressed the now fully alert travelers. "I finally have some good news— landing news. Now, before you start picking out your home sites, let me tell you that we are approaching the planet in which we hope to land. However, it's still a couple of weeks away. At our current speed we still probably have a million miles more to go. We have to start decreasing our speed, otherwise, at our current rate, we would fly right into another void. However, we have to do this slowly; otherwise we will burn up as we enter the atmosphere of this new system. When we get into their atmosphere this plane will start to get hot, you will see brilliant light outside your windows. I recommend that you do not stare into that light. We'll be like a fireball. The heat shields developed by those who built our heat conduit systems back in Zavre should help us considerably but we could experience a major temperature increase. We have coolant pumps available but we don't know how efficient they are. This will help somewhat but don't expect to be real cool. Drink water to prevent heat prostration or kidney problems. If there is a problem let us know. We will do the best we can. Once again, if you have any questions, let us know."

During the next week, the cabin was filled with excitement. The passengers finally saw an end to this extended trip. And then Yari approached Eve, "I believe I saw a planet closer than the one you suggest. It is on the outer rim of the sun and probably a week closer. Shouldn't we head for that?"

"I saw that planet some time ago. It's not for us. It's a dead planet like the dead moons that encircled Zavre. One has no atmosphere while the others have surface temperatures that we couldn't survive. It would be a disaster if we chose that one. Let's go with the original plans."

That day, with Yari and Eve's approval, Jonah blasted off the last of his battery brakes. The speed of the ship slowed down noticeably and as expected the temperature inside the vessel went up considerably. The heat shield glowed white hot as the rocket entered the atmosphere of the planet they hoped to call home.

CHAPTER XXXI

Two days later, with the ship still traveling at almost seven hundred miles an hour and five hundred thousand miles from its target, Yari called his brain trust together; "Guys, this is what I plan to do. You better agree with me since I have no other ideas. One, I'm still traveling too fast for any type of a landing. Number two, I am planning to spin around the planet that Eve has designated as the landing spot. In doing this, I should lose speed and also get a look at the ground cover. I hope it's not all mountainous or water. Our passengers should be aware that the temperature in the cabin could get uncomfortably warm. Be prepared for some major complaints. The cooling elements will help but not by much. Three, if I don't reduce the speed of this baby by a lot and get the right trajectory, the ship will disintegrate on landing. I don't think we want to do that after we've gone so far."

Eve, Jonah and Adam looked at each other as if they had an answer to their pilot's request for help. They had none. Adam finally answered, "Yari, everything that you've said sounds logical to me. As the air builds up in the atmosphere we should develop greater resistance and that should decrease our speed. Going around the planet a couple of flybys is a great idea. What do you say to that, Eve?"

"I'm for it one hundred percent. It'll give me a chance to look at the surface to see what we're heading for. I've already pretty sure that it's about sixty percent water so there's land to land on, Yari, so don't fear. How much land-mass is another question, but I'll let you know even after the first pass. I'd suggest that you consider three or four passes so we can get a real good look. By that time the speed of the ship should be more reasonable."

"Yari, how are your other pilots doing? Are they on target?"

"Don't know, Eve. When we entered this atmosphere we lost contact. They may try to land near us but I think they'll end up on a different part of the planet. Otherwise, they are okay."

The next day, with the ship looking like a piece of white lightning due to its speed, Yari muttered to himself, *thank God for the ceramic heat shields that Davis incorporated all around the ship.* But even with the most efficient heat shield and the cooling system on, the temperature in the cabin rose considerably and Adam could understand the passengers' discomfort.

After much discussion on the speaker system, it was universally agreed that at any temperature beyond 120° the Captain would put the cooling system on high. It was not the most efficient system but it did lower the temperature slightly.

The following day, after two passes around the new planet, with the ship slowing considerably, Eve announced, "Okay, I got a great view of this new planet. There's a lot of water, it appears like 60 to 80 percent water, but plenty of land-mass for us to shoot for. I saw an area that looks like flat land that lies near some river or water site. This could be the spot for a landing. Yari, I'll give you the coordinates on your next go around." All Yari did was moan; it was difficult enough to keep the ship on a general target let alone to spot a landing. They were still traveling much too fast..

On the next pass around the planet, with the reversals up and the full flaps down the speed dropped to 250 miles per hour, Yari, trying his utmost to keep the nose of the ship up, had to announce, "Guys, I'll never be able to hold this ship's head up much longer. On the next go around, I'm going to drop the landing gear which should help in slowing down the ship and head for the spot that Eve picked. At the speed we are traveling, I hope that the landing wheels are not torn off. If my speed is not drastically reduced, I'd rather not think what will happen if we touch down at a bad angle.

"Is there anything we can do?"

"Jonah, do you have anything left in your brake batteries? That could help."

"I think they gave me all the juice they had, but I'll press their restart button again and hope for the best."

Jonah pressed the button that controlled the last two batteries that had previously acted as brakes.

Much to Jonah's surprise, and the surprise of the rest of the crew, they felt the ship shudder slightly and then slow enough to be noticed. Eve screamed with delight as they all looked at Yari and his instruments. "You're my man, Jonah; the ship is now traveling 200 miles per hour. By the time we go around once more it should be below 175. I'm goin' to drop the brakes fully on the next go around and if the speed drops to 140, I'll release the landing wheels. If the wheels are not torn off altogether, we may have a chance. We're not going to have the smoothest landing but who the hell cares. We may slide and roll two miles, but we will be landed. I hope we don't overshoot the land area and land in the water. I pray, Eve, that there will be air for me to breath."

"From what my instruments show me, Yari, if we get there, there will be air. I would suggest, however, that we wear our oxygen masks when we first step on the ground."

"If we step on the ground," Jonah replied, without a smile.

Still traveling at speeds faster than designed, the ship Archangel landed hard on the earth, bounced, skidded and then rolled almost two miles down a flat desert and through a river with such force as to almost demolish it. The landing wheels collapsed and blew apart on the force of the landing. Exploding through the desert with a roar, it continued through another rocky area, some additional water and then half way up a small incline, it finally stopped in a cloud of dust and sand.

Yari Roebling was killed instantly. Landing at that excess speed, the front of the ship just collapsed. Six people in the far back seats, still in their seat belts, drowned as the tail of the plane broke off into the first water hazard. Unfortunately, it was in the rear storage compartments that contained all the books and documents on the sciences, literature, music and art of Zavre were stored; this was all lost. The fifteen thousand years of history and culture of Zavre was destroyed in an instant.

Noah Jacobs was thrown off the plane into the water where he floated to the surface. Jonah, sitting behind Roebling, was thrown into the water and was last seen trying to swim to safety. Eve and Adam and the remaining passengers survived. As they exited the ship, they cautiously removed their air masks and were delighted to discover, as Eve had prayed, that the new planet had air they could breath.

They never saw remnants of the other two ships.

#

For the next years, the survivors stayed in the desert area. They had landed in a country filled with wild animals and nomadic, uncivilized people living in small tribes praying to idols and the stars. It was there that they intermarried and raised their families. As time passed they traveled to the plains of the junction of two rivers where they settled and tried to restart their lives. Within a generation many contacted a disease that was unknown to the people of Zavre. Eve and Adam survived and had two children, Abraham and Sarah.

EPILOGUE

When time is not measured in years but in seasons and natural and human events, eons pass by quickly. Hundreds and then thousands of years passed and the stories, history and culture of the people of Zavre who traveled on the great ship Archangel were related by word of mouth, generation to generation. Many, if not all of their stories were lost in translation and exaggeration.

The technology, science and knowledge that the travelers on the great ship took with them were tragically lost during the thousand of centuries that followed.

The story of the great Ark became a part of our history. The stories of Adam and Eve and of Noah, and Jonah were embellished in succeeding generations. Their story joined other legends and tales in a way those people could not have planned or envisioned. Some even became our prophets.

CPSIA information can be obtained
at www.ICGtesting.com
Printed in the USA
BVHW031700040820
585465BV00001B/10

9 781984 58311